BLACK BOOKS

SAN FRANCISCO AUTHORS SERIES:

Vertical Intercourse, by Paul Reed

Vertical Intercourse

by the same author:

FICTION

Facing It
Longing
Vertical Intercourse

NONFICTION

Serenity
How To Persuade Your Lover To Use a Condom
Serenity: Second Revised Edition
The Q Journal
The Savage Garden
Back from the Brink (chapbook)
The Redwood Diary

EROTICA
(writing as Max Exander)

ManSex
SafeStud
LoveSex
LeatherSex
Deeds of the Night

HUMOR
Cats Are from Jupiter, Dogs Are from Pluto

ZINES
(co-edited with Michael Johnstone)

Rant & Rave

VERTICAL INTERCOURSE

PAUL REED

BLACK BOOKS
san francisco

Grateful acknowledgment is made for the generous support of the following institutions and individuals: PEN American Center; The Friends of William D. Trumbo Foundation; Patti Breitman; Jane Meadows; Rudd and Gerry; and, of course Kevin and always Matt.

VERTICAL INTERCOURSE. Copyright © 2000 by Paul Reed. All rights reserved. No part of this book may be used or reproduced in any manner whatsoever without written permission, except in the case of brief quotations embodied in critical articles or reviews. For information, write Black Books, Post Office Box 31155, San Francisco, CA 94131-0155.

Cover and text design by the author and Image Comp, San Francisco
Cover and title page photo by Michael W. Sauer, 1999
Photo model: Jason Mannino
Author photo by Steve Savage
Composition by Jeff Brandenburg, San Francisco
Set in Ehrhardt MT

Library of Congress Cataloging-in-Publication Data

Reed, Paul, 1956–
   Vertical intercourse : a novel / Paul Reed.
      p.   cm.
   ISBN 1-892723-06-9
   1. Gay men—Fiction. 2. San Francisco (Calif.)—Fiction. I. Title.
   PS3568.E369 V47 2000
   813'.54—dc21   00-010114

Printed in Canada

FIRST EDITION 2000
2 4 6 8 0 9 7 5 3 1

for David Charlsen
IN MEMORY

VERTICAL INTERCOURSE

1

It is almost always cold in San Francisco, especially in the summer, when the dry heat of California's Great Central Valley sucks the moisture off the Pacific Ocean, off San Francisco Bay, as if dying of thirst. The result of this ecology is that thick, roiling fog rushes towards the California Delta and obscures everything in its path — that everything includes San Francisco.

And this is where I am: San Francisco, city of sin, or, in the words of the grand old dame in the movie *San Francisco*, the "wickedest city on earth." It doesn't feel very wicked or very sinful, as I sit here at Just Desserts on Church Street, drinking my cup of tea, eating a walnut cookie, and contemplating life. It does feel cold. Every time someone opens the front door, a blast of cold wind rushes in, forcing me, and other patrons, to keep our sweaters on. After all, it is July.

I am sitting and thinking about life. My life, that is. I've always been so self-centered that I can't concern myself with the lives of others. Matter of fact, I rarely think about other people, except for such superficial thoughts as: Are they good looking? Smart? Intriguing? Could I have sex with him, or her?

Lately, I haven't been feeling very well, mostly emotionally. Dark moods have decided that I am to be their plaything, tossing me around like a giant beach ball in the surf on a cold winter's day in the middle of a horrific thunderstorm. This is nothing particularly new for me, since I've spent nearly fifteen years in therapy — nine years with Josef Barkman, one year with Hilda Kesselhoff, two years with Lisa Tannenbaum, and occasional mental health consultations with Edgar Horstmann. That comes to thirteen years, I know, but there were years, two to be precise, when I was "between therapists," as I like to say.

And now I have a new one, Dr. Emma Kiljoy. I am passing time here before our first session. The tea will bolster my spirits subtly, and the cookie will satisfy my always growling stomach. I need fortification. First meetings with therapists are rather lackluster and nervous-making. There's all that business about getting to know them, letting them get to know you, and finding a regular appointment time that is convenient for both. I am on edge. Will this term of therapy prove useful? Or am I about to launch myself into a grand waste of time and money?

But I do need some help, some guidance. I've made it through Valium, Ativan, Xanax, food, cigarettes, and Percocet. I've done AA, NA, CODA, and OA. I've survived Christianity, higher education, and golf. I'm a mess.

And I'm going to be forty next year.

Finishing my cookie and washing it down with the last swallow of tea, I take a deep breath and begin the walk from

Church Street to Dr. Kiljoy's office on Noe Street. It is windy, as usual, and a little chilly under the thick branches of the trees that overhang the streets of the Duboce Triangle. I see that up ahead I'm going to pass The Professor, one of the neighborhood's many resident homeless nuts. He is so-called because he always carries a thick sheaf of papers as he wanders the streets, lecturing in a near-shout, to no one, about Roman antiquity and the Caesars. At the edge of the clearing that is Duboce Park, I look up and see the dark mass of fog in the western sky. I should have worn a heavier jacket, a sweater is not enough.

As soon as I enter the waiting room of the Victorian house-turned-analysts'-offices, Dr. Kiljoy opens a door, smiles, and beckons me inside. She appears to be the most glamorous of all the therapists I've had — tall but slender (imperious would be the right word), dressed in a brown linen suit, her hair a deep amber styled into what is called a pageboy cut, or, more accurately, I think, a Cleopatra.

Her office is certainly faithful to stereotypes about psychotherapy — long windows looking across the cityscape, framed in velvet umber curtains. The inviting, soft couch with a pillow at one end (I've never done therapy lying down, though, with the therapist behind me. That has always seemed too Viennese). Her chair — beside a small table and a large mahogany desk (intricately and overwhelmingly carved) — is, of course, high-backed, overstuffed, and upholstered in rich brown leather. A tastefully muted Persian rug on the floor. Framed etchings on the walls — dark European scenes that can barely be discerned in the dim, comforting light of the room. Fresh cut flowers. And volumes of books.

I've been through this get-acquainted process more than once, of course, and I am not looking forward to the initial visits with Dr. Kiljoy. I'll have to revisit my childhood, re-examine my adolescence, and fill in all the details of my adult life, too. This prospect terrifies, as though it were some kind of audition. For all I know, it might be. After all, what does a therapist do if they encounter a patient who makes them cringe? Whose voice or mannerisms grate on their nerves such that they would rather strangle than help the poor fool? Do they refer the patient to someone else? Or do they plod on, trying to overlook the annoyances?

After a few preliminaries at the outset — How are you? . . . Fine . . . What a handsome office . . . Nice view, too . . . Why, thank you . . . Won't you please have a seat? — we begin, as my mother used to say, to get down to brass tacks. She asks me why I've decided to see her, what brings me here. I tell her that I haven't been feeling quite right for a long time.

"How long have you felt unwell?" she asks.

"About thirty years," I say.

She smiles. "That's not uncommon for people who are depressed."

"Well, I'm not sure I'm depressed," I say. "And I'm not really sure that 'unwell' is the right word. It's more like a general malaise, not feeling myself. In the past, I think the word 'malingering' would describe it."

"That's not uncommon, either," she says, "in this time of epidemic."

I am a little taken aback by this observation, since I haven't said anything about my health or circumstances or anything for that matter. Do I look so queer? It is, I decide, I hope, an invitation to disclose all the details of my health status, but this is not the reason I've decided to start therapy again. My serostatus is beside the point.

But what the hell.

"Funny you should say that," I say. "Every time I see my doctor and tell him I'm not feeling very well, he reminds me that I was supposed to have been dead years ago, so what do I expect?"

Dr. Kiljoy nods, as if this were wisdom.

I take a deep breath and go on. "But that's not why I've come to see you. It's more complicated than that, and I don't think my HIV status has much to do with it . . . Of course I agree that might have something to do with how I've been feeling, because . . . you know . . . life used to be much simpler, much easier . . . Oh, I'm not making any sense."

She nods patiently and makes a face that I take to be intended as an expression of therapeutic concern — a slight tilting of the head to one side, a pursing of the lips, and a puppy-sad wrinkling around the eyes. What I notice most about this mannerism is that it allows an unshadowed view of her very wrinkled neck, which looks about the same as one of those Chinese dogs that have no hair, just folds of flesh.

"And how long have you felt this way," she asks in a near whisper, the perfect picture of the concerned, attentive therapist.

"Well, it seemed to start just about the time Gardenia got sick. Oh, I mean Michael-Gardenia," I explain. "He's a friend I met a few years ago, and of course we all have girl names . . . well, some of us do, but that's . . . well, I guess I'll just say Michael. . . .

"Anyway, when she . . . I mean he . . . got sick, I found myself enjoying life a little less. Bit by bit it's gotten harder and harder to do things I used to love to do, like going hiking or going to a movie. Stuff like that. I'm in despair about it all, this malaise, this feeling that everything has become too difficult. And, to jump to another topic, I'm not getting any younger, and that is taking a real toll on me, my self-esteem, my plans for the future . . . I'm rambling, aren't I?"

She nods but says nothing. She picks up a pen and notebook from the table beside her chair and begins writing something down. I find this to be a curious thing to do so early in the session. What is she writing — Mania, or Psychosis, or Narcissism, or Depression, or Recommend Shock Therapy? Or is it something more personal — Pick up the Dry Cleaning, or Don't Forget to Buy Preparation H?

I take another deep breath (how many have I taken today?). Her office seems to lack an adequate oxygen supply. Her silence and her stare make me uncomfortable, as though I am being scrutinized by a potential employer, or am on a date with someone who has absolutely nothing to say.

Finally, after a silence of a few seconds — which feel like several minutes — she speaks: "The term for what you are describing is 'anhedonia,' the inability to experience pleasure. It's common in depression."

She gives me a sympathetic little smile. That's when I realize that already I feel a little disgusted. Not again, I say to myself, another sympathetic therapist, probably completely disingenuous. But, I reprimand myself, I should give it a chance. Perhaps she's not like the others. Perhaps she really is concerned. Perhaps I won't represent the monthly payment on her Mercedes.

After another expanding silence, she shifts in her chair, as if to break wind, and asks, "Have you many friends?"

How can I answer? This question, so often asked by doctors and nurses and intake counselors and mothers and long-distance friends, always stumps me. But I do my best: "Uh, well . . . yes and no . . . I had a lot of friends. But the number has been reduced by attrition . . . you know, a bunch of them died from, first, AIDS, then from AZT poisoning. Another bunch died from OD-ing on junk. Others moved away. But there are a lot of people around me, who I consider friends, or potential friends, and a couple very close ones."

I pause, losing my train of thought, and then: "But these are mostly new friends, something like the third or fourth generation of friends. No one I know now is the original group I met when I moved here in 1980.

"That's one of the things that's bothering me, that I've lost all the witnesses . . . well, most of the witnesses to my life. I mean we used to sit around drinking espresso and daydream about what we wanted to become, what we wanted to accomplish. I remember Tom always wanted to be a real estate mogul, and Edward a musician, and Cap a designer, and Richard a writer—"

"And what about you?" she asks.

"I wanted to be an editor, and here I am. But they're all gone now. There's no one to see that I made it, that I got where I wanted to go. No one, that is, who'd remember me at twenty-three, full of hopes and ambitions."

"Do you have any romantic interests? A boyfriend?"

I screw my face up in a grimace. Romance is a touchy subject with me. I've buried three lovers and gone now for several years without. "I'm not sure," I answer. "Lately I've been 'chatting' on the computer with a guy by the handle 'Anson,' but we haven't progressed to actually speaking on the phone or meeting each other. But we have had online sex, if you know what I mean."

She nods that she understands.

"I've been thinking about asking to meet him, but I just haven't had the nerve, not yet. But there is a definite interest in each other, I can tell that. And there's sexual tension and lots of flirtation. Kind of weird, isn't it, this online world."

Another silence stretches between us. I wonder if this is something I truly want to be doing, talking to a strange woman in a strange room, looking out over the skyline of San Francisco and discussing sex and romance online. Finally, by way of breaking the silence and changing the subject, I say, "I suppose you'd probably like me to start at the beginning, my background and childhood and all that?"

She nods and says, "That would be helpful."

And so I recite the general facts of my life: born in San Diego, that sleepy city of retired admirals, golf, and prescription sunglasses; raised just to the north, in La Jolla; college and graduate school at Stanford; the commencement of my adult life in San Francisco, the editing job, the late nights, fog, wind, disco, punk, and sex.

She scribbles in her notebook.

I go on: "I was raised as a Baptist, which probably explains just about everything for you. I've had my flirtations with drugs and drink, even developed a problem with downers. I used to believe that life was going to be grand . . . travel, adventures, drunken parties, incessant sex. I'd watch TV as a kid and just yearn to be part of the glamour I saw on Johnny Carson, Merv Griffin. My favorite programs were *Dark Shadows* and *Bonanza* . . . I had a big crush on the character Adam. I guess I watched too much TV.

"What else? My father sold insurance, my mother was executive secretary of the local Chamber of Commerce, and of my two sisters and two brothers, my favorite was my oldest brother Jake. I've had a crush on him as long as I can remember. Now he sells real estate and lives in Walnut Creek. I've had three lovers, all of whom I've buried. No boyfriends since then, just a weird single life with the occasional pickup or late-night visit to a sex club. Grief is everywhere in my life . . . you could call me the black widow. And as I said, I'm not sure at all what's developing with Anson."

This recitation, I assume, is to be the beginning (for the umpteenth time) of yet another probing of the caverns of memory. Therapists love this kind of stuff, as though, by poking around these dark caverns, the dim beam of the flashlight of exploration might suddenly illuminate a stalactite or two with clear and unmistakable markings: Things Your Parents Did Wrong, or Why You Are Fucked Up.

Much as I don't want to revisit all this childhood stuff, I am aware, however reluctantly, that it is an essential and necessary part of therapeutic process. It's plain to see, I think, as I blather on about the piano lessons I received in Los Angeles (the promising protégé) that any therapist can't help a person if that person is completely unknown. On what can a therapist base their analysis? Their ideas about the nature of the problem? Their supposed helpfulness?

So I talk on, in greater detail: anthropology, history, and philosophy at Stanford, master's degrees, a failed doctorate, the abandonment of music as a career choice. The wild sex life of San Francisco in the early eighties, the days of dating and faithfulness (called, I believe, "serial monogamy"), the sick friends, the dying, the sword of Damocles and all that miserable stuff that came along with the epidemic like a baggage car on a train speeding recklessly, in the middle of the night, toward a breach in the rails . . .

This last simile, I realize, is a bit too Ayn Rand for even my tastes, so I stop talking, rather suddenly, and my therapist looks puzzled for a moment, until she understands that I am tired of my own accounting.

"Is there any more?" she asks.

"Of course, I could go on and on, but that's the general outline of my life."

She nods. "It's about time to start wrapping it up for today. I think that I can help you, if you agree to continue . . ."

"Well, I'm not sure I've said anything, or can say anything that matters—"

"But you've already told me one very important thing that your current depression and soul-searching coincided with your friend Michael's illness."

She pauses, lets this observation sink in. I'm not impressed; of course I feel bad about Michael's health. I say so.

"But my point," she says, "is that it has added just the little extra amount of stress to your life that pushes everything past the edge of tolerability. Can you see that?"

God, she can be pompous, I think. I'll have to watch that I don't let her authoritative manner intimidate me. I say, "I see your point. Of course it's just that so many feelings, so many issues . . . just so much has come up for attention, I don't know where to start—"

"This is a good start," she cuts in.

I lower my eyes, study the patterns in the Persian rug, and let silence fill the room. Then I say, "But these problems . . .

these things that are bothering me . . . are very real. I don't think I could rank them and say 'this is the most unsettling' or 'that is the real problem.' To repeat myself, I'm just terribly confused.

"Oh, and did I mention that I'm going to be forty next year?"

She nods, makes a note. "Our time is up for today."

This irritates me, a little shock of memory from earlier therapy — the making of fifty minutes into a one-hour session. Fifty minutes has always seemed too brief. How can anyone get to know another in just fifty minutes a week? It is an expensive proposition, one that gives rise to at least a smidgen of suspicion that therapy is, essentially, about long-term financing.

Don't be so cynical, I tell myself. So I ask about the details of payment, insurance claims, and so on. And then she says, "I really think I'll be able to be of some help to you. Shall we meet again next week, same time?"

"Yes, all right," I mumble, feeling quite uncertain of myself, my motives, and the darkness that compels me to seek some sort of emotional assistance.

When I emerge from her office, it feels, short as the session was, that I've been there for hours. The afternoon sea breeze has kicked up and is pushing fog over Twin Peaks and down into Eureka Valley. Icy and cutting, the harsh wind seems always a slap in the face, one of the few things I dislike about San Francisco. The wind cuts through my sweater. Now I'm really cold.

I brace myself and walk towards Market Street, intending to stop at Cafe Flore for a cup of plain, black coffee. But as usual, there is no place to sit, and the crowd is so obnoxiously hip, slick, and cool that I decide the best thing is to go home and go to sleep. I took the afternoon off for this first session, so I may as well take advantage of the down time to get some rest.

As I walk, I am hit up for spare change six times, read a sign pinned to the filthy jacket of a sleeping homeless man that reads Veteran, Please Help. When I get to my apartment, I have to step over a woman who is passed out at the foot of the stairs leading up to my front door. I note, as I reach into my pocket for my keys, that there is a stream of urine on the sidewalk trailing back to the front of the woman's jeans.

There are messages on my machine. Instead of heading straight for the bed, and the oblivion of a nap, I punch the play button. "Hey, it's me, Michael, doing okay I guess, talk to you later." The second message, "Hello, pumpkin, it's Charlton just calling to check in, give me a call soon."

I decide to call them back later. I put The Smiths on the stereo, on low volume, lay down, and quickly fall asleep.

2

It was Charlton who recommended Dr. Kiljoy to me, and it was from him that I learned all that I knew of her. Attempting to get personal information out of one's therapist, I know, is like pulling teeth. They believe that the developing relationship between the therapist and client must be done outside the parameters of bias. Intimacy, personal facts — these can interfere with the relationship. It is in witnessing how this patient-therapist relationship develops that therapists learn a great deal about their clients.

From Charlton I learned that Dr. Kiljoy was the daughter of Jewish intellectuals who had perished in the chambers of Bergen-Belsen. Just a small child, she had been sent to live with her aunt in Paris, and they managed, miraculously, to escape to America just as France was being occupied.

I was not surprised by this biography, for Dr. Kiljoy seemed, indeed, to carry the dark burden of people whose lives have been directly touched by the Holocaust.

I learned, too, that she had been married for twenty-five years until she was widowed at the age of 46. Charlton knew little else about the marriage. He had met her when in the hospital for chemotherapy, and he saw her as a patient for a year after his remission. She had been, he said, a tremendous help.

When I told him, one day over lunch, that I feared I was becoming alarmingly depressed — or, too depressed, as depression has always haunted me — he said, "You must see Emma Kiljoy. Here's her number. She helped me a great deal when I got out of the hospital. The doctors — those quacks — had given me two to three years, at most, and I was desperate to talk to someone.

"She had been on staff at the hospital — a sort of roving therapist — and when I first laid eyes on her, I knew that I'd have to see her, to have her hear me out. That elegant hair, the wrinkles of wisdom at the corners of those chocolate brown eyes, the way she carries herself with such somber dignity — all these things aroused in me some wondrous, instant trust. And so I became her patient."

"That's quite a recommendation," I said. "I'll call her. What do I have to lose? You've never steered me wrong."

And so I had gone home and left a message on her voicemail. That was three weeks ago, and now I have had my first session with her and see what Charlton meant. Her bearing is regal, her voice firm and steady, yet soothing. Had I any heterosexual tendencies (as I must somewhere within me), I might well develop an obsession with her.

When I wake from my nap, I phone Charlton. "Well, I saw your beloved and eminent Dr. Kiljoy today."

"How did it go?" he asked. "Do you think you'll be able to work with her?"

"I think so," I said. "She is as formidable as you said, and I was taken with her in a way. Of course I also felt contempt at the same time, because I have such a love/hate thing with therapists, with therapy. I can't help but notice any flaw, and I'm deeply suspicious."

"Oh, don't worry," he said. "You'll come to trust her soon enough, and then you can get down to some real work. It's not easy, these days, I know—"

"You're lapsing into clichés again, dear," I chastise him. We move on to other topics — the chill of the summer fog, the news story about the alligator missing from the zoo, the pitiful and overdeveloped state of the Castro district. But we are most concerned with Michael's illness and his seeming downhill slide.

"I haven't seen him in about a week and a half," I say. "I guess I should go over there, but I'm afraid to watch him decline. It's really upsetting to me—"

"Well, dear, if you think it's upsetting to you," Charlton says, "think how Michael must feel."

"Oh, yeah," I say, "my old self-centeredness rears its ugly head again.

"You said it, not me," he says. "But getting back to the subject — not you — I took Michael to the doctor on Tuesday, and even though he looked quite awful, he seemed to have plenty of energy. He was feisty with the receptionist and was trying to cruise a cute little shaved-headed guy in the waiting room. I'd say he's okay for the moment."

"But I'm not imagining, am I, that he's getting worse?" I ask.

Charlton takes a deep breath, then says, "No, you're not imagining it. He's lost more weight, and the MAC is acting up, giving him high fevers. He seems to have grown resistant to the drugs for MAC."

"I wonder if he'll last much longer," I say.

I met Charlton at work. He's a freelance book designer, a renowned colorist, and we immediately took a liking to each other. It was never anything romantic, and our fondness for each other grew over a period of years. Now I count him among my best of friends. For a long time he had a long-distance lover, Duncan, in New York. But for reasons I was never able to fully discern, they had drifted apart. It was a great blow to Charlton, but he was not very forthcoming about it all, so I never pressed him. Lately, he'd been dating a staggeringly handsome young man — boy, really — by the name of Derek something-or-other. I have yet to meet this blond beauty.

Charlton is a mix of complex emotions and moods, and his history is filled with celebrities, magnificent dinner parties, and world travel. Yet he retains a beguiling simplicity, living close to the bone. With his career and reputation, he could easily be extraordinarily highfalutin, yet he remains completely grounded, never allowing any of his glittering lifestyle to go to his head.

He has been ill — twice — with ghastly lymphoma, not AIDS related. He survived to outlive his doctor's grim prognoses, and for this reason alone he cherishes life while at the same time — having met his mortality face to face — realizing that it amounts, in the end, to nothing. Cliché or not, to Charlton life is to be lived in the moment. It can be snuffed out in an instant.

Because of this, he makes a point of always caring for sick friends. Antibody negative, he has seen generations of his friends and colleagues pass away, wave after wave, while he's been left, curiously, behind. The pandemic has taken its emotional toll, yet he triumphs over the tragedy by caring for the ill. Lately, he has been helping Michael, bringing lunches and dinners — tender meatloaf, steaming hot-and-sour soup, ice creams, sorbets. Rallying around Michael we all become stronger, closer. It seems clear that Michael has very little time left, and we reconcile ourselves to this impending loss and do what we can to make his final time comfortable and full of love.

It is night, and I'm walking the streets of the Castro, a constitutional stroll you might call it. The fog has rolled in, thick and heavy, and a gusty westerly wind whips at my face, my jacket. I walk past Michael's flat, but I do not stop. Not without calling. He needs his rest and doesn't need unannounced visitors. Or am I just afraid to stop by? Afraid to see Michael in a bad way? I really should do more, I tell myself. I should be taking Michael to the doctor. I should be bringing him soup and animal crackers.

But I just can't. I think I've got what they call 'compassion fatigue.' I'm just plain worn out with illness and dying.

Thankfully, luckily, wondrously, the new therapies have snatched many friends and acquaintances back from the brink. But not Michael.

I reflect on the afternoon, on the first therapy session. Will it prove to be a help? What's wrong with me anyway? Why can't I just snap out of it? Why this heaviness? Why this surging of despair, this loneliness, this upwelling of sadness?

I surrender myself to the cold wind, allowing it to wash over and through me, to serve as a cleansing for my spirit. Perhaps there is hope yet. There is always hope.

I met Michael years and years ago, after the first wave of death had shuddered through town. We were both walking our dogs one evening. How bourgeois, I thought, as he struck up a conversation with me. This was in the days right on the edge of the homeless/beggar thing, so you could actually walk outdoors without being harassed every ten feet. And it was before the next ice age reached the coast of central California; it was possible to linger on the sidewalk and talk to somebody new. Now, of course, you just stare at the sidewalk and frown a lot. A mean, uncaring expression is the best guard against beggars, kooks, nut cases, meter maids, bashers, tweakers, and gym bunnies — all the wildlife of the Castro.

We were clearly flirting with each other, ostensibly talking about our dogs — he had a collie and I a cocker spaniel — but the subtext was something like: *Does he like me? He's cute. I wonder if he has a big dick? How can I lure him home?*

After the usual exchange of nonsense about cups of coffee and conversation, we decided to go to my place, because he said that the plaster in his ceiling had cracked during the last big earthquake and was now coming down in chunks. He never knew when another chunk was going to fall, so it was a bit dangerous.

"Why not get the landlord to fix it?" I asked, but he explained that the landlady was an old Burmese woman who always acted as if she couldn't speak English, except, of course, when he was late with the rent.

As we walked towards my flat, he told me a little bit about himself: He collected lunch boxes and back issues of MAD magazine. He was "between boyfriends." He was going to have a root canal the next day. He loved Phoebe Snow, Jane Olivor, Alien Sex Fiend, and Depeche Mode (I tried to compose a mental picture of the kind of person who could follow a Depeche Mode CD with one of Jane Olivor, but I couldn't do it).

After some groping and gasping, some push and pull, standing-up sex, we collapsed on my bed and lay panting. I knew then that we were not going to be lovers, but best friends. He knew it, too. The requisite spark hadn't been there. We went out to Lupann's for dinner, and made fast friends.

Michael had tested positive in 1985, by which time he had already experienced thrush and swollen lymph nodes. He continued to work and take care of himself for the next decade, biding his time for a treatment that would work.

Now he has failed the new therapies (it has been a horror story of drug toxicities and liver failure) and has no options other than to wait. But the course of his illness is a downward slope, a little worse every month. Of course everyone around him tries to encourage him to plunge into the netherworld of alternative treatments. Thomas, Michael's lover, has resigned himself to the negative prognosis and no longer fusses. Charlton, a two-time survivor of lymphoma, has tried to convince Michael that alternative therapies can indeed be quite helpful. Charlton himself had defeated the lymphoma with a combination of holism, macrobiotics, and low-dose chemotherapy. Mad Mama Jones, Michael's live-in volunteer home nursing aide, steers well clear of it all, deferring to her "client ethics" as a caregiver. (She thinks, secretly, however, that Michael is being a stubborn ass. But she doesn't say this, of course.)

Most vocal among our group are Scotty and Kent (boyfriends who share my flat), who bring brochures, books, and bagsful of supplements to Michael's bedside.

But Michael is stubborn. He'll have none of it — an attitude that has prompted a number of small but anguished quarrels. "Girl, I tell you," I said on the phone recently, "you are the classic AIDS victim."

"What does that mean?" he asked, crossly.

"You're still operating under the old rules of illness. You've swallowed the whole role of the longsuffering AIDS patient — I guess I should use the throwback acronym PWA — you've swallowed it hook, line, and sinker . . . I'm surprised you don't have a pair of AZT earrings. Those old blue-and-white capsules are positively antique now—"

Michael had hung up on me then. It isn't so much that we all believe in the possibility of some New Age miracle as it is that Michael has obviously given up, a difficult thing to witness. Now, whenever I think that I should call him and give him another good talking to, I remind myself that he's a grown man, he can make his own decisions. He's capable of weighing risks and benefits of treatments, including no treatment at all. Granted, the new therapies have failed him, but he has given up entirely. For me to pursue it further would only inflict unnecessary cruelty.

When I get home from my walk, I log onto the computer, hoping that Anson has sent some e-mail or is even online.

Yes, e-mail! *Just writing to say I've been enjoying 'talking' with you online, and I think it's about time we got together to meet in person. What do you say?*

This short message sends me into a tailspin, a good kind of tailspin, exciting. It's been a long dry spell since my last boyfriend — an aborted attempt at "opening myself up" to a new "relationship" after the grief of losing Edward. And of course, this message makes me a wreck. I know it's time for us to meet. If we don't meet soon — and see if we even like each other, or have any chemistry at all — then this online flirtation will undoubtedly fizzle out. That's what happens if you let the crucial moment go by. A matter of timing.

I send my reply: *I agree that it's time we meet face to face. Where and when? Lunch? Dinner? Drinks?*

Not very clever, this reply, but clear and direct. Clear and direct are better qualities than cleverness. I don't want to appear too eager, because that might read like desperation. But the fact is that I am ecstatic. Finally, at long last, a date! Facing forty years next birthday, I've been wondering if this long dry spell might blister into some withering bitterness, making me a curmudgeonly middle-aged man grumbling about the weather, rain or shine.

While I sit at my computer, staring at the list of guys online, Anson appears. He spots me and we go off into a private room to chat. *So, did you get my e-mail?* he writes. *Whatta you think? It's time, isn't it?*

I write: *I sent you a reply, check your mail.*

He leaves the room momentarily to check his mail, then returns and writes: *I like dinner best. I don't drink. And lunch is too much a crunch for me, going to school and all. But dinner would be fine. Are you free next Friday night?*

I glance at my datebook. *Yes, okay, next Friday, about half past seven? At the no-name restaurant?*

Cool, he answers. Then we start in:

ANSON: *It was a rotten day at work, of course, it always is, but I was looking forward to getting an answer from you about getting together, and that made the afternoon bearable.*

ME: *I'm flattered. Did you rub your crotch when you thought about me?*

Oh, the temerity! But this is the unreal world of the Internet, life lived online.

ANSON: *Did I ever. It made me horny, thinking that we're finally going to meet and thinking about all the dirty things we've done with each other through the computer. And we haven't even gone to voice yet. And it looks like we're not going to go to voice, since we've already set up our date here, now. You won't have any trouble telling who's me. I'll be the boy with the shaved head and the unearthly green eyes—*

ME: *I remember your description of your looks, but a shaved head boy is hardly a rarity anymore. Maybe during ACT UP days, when I first started shaving my head, but not now. I think it's great, because boys with shaved heads are so much cuter than hair boys. Don't you think? I always say that everyone looks better (1) tied up, (2) with a shaved head, and (3) with a dick in their mouth.*

ANSON: *I agree, I agree. Between the two of us, with two shaved heads, we'll look like a couple of giant phalluses gulping down our Caesar salad and pommes frites.*

ME: *I hate French . . .*

ANSON: *Sorry, mon petite homme.*

ME: *Gag! :(*

ANSON: *Ah, come on and smile for me :) I can't wait to get that big thing in my mouth.*

ME: *And vice-versa . . .*

ANSON: *We're running down. Time to cruise other boys . . .*

ME: *Bye.*

❖

When I log off, I am so fired up by our exchange that I know I have to go out catting around. I drive to the dirty bookstore on Folsom Street, enter the peep show arcade, and, miraculously, the center booth of three connecting booths with glory holes is actually vacant. I occupy it at once.

Peeking through the hole to my right, I see a large, bearded man with a short, fat dick sticking out of his jeans. No thanks. Through the hole to my left, I see what appears to be a very cute Latin boy, stroking an absolutely enormous cock, perhaps one of the biggest ones I've ever seen.

I have to have it. Of course. It's a man thing, this drive for volume, for more, for greater and greater inches, for more and more encounters. I beckon to him and he starts to push it through the glory hole, but it's so thick that he really has to shove to get it through.

Hmm, I think, I'm going to have to pull out all the stops for this thing — mouth, hands, tongue, throat. It will be real workout, a delicious, luscious, extravagant taste of heaven. The taste of boys. The taste of men.

The weekend arrives. I decide that no matter what, it's time for me to visit Michael and get back into the habit of helping with his caregiving. There is great resistance in me, a feeling of doom, knowing that Michael will probably die soon, wondering why, yet again, I must anticipate another loss. I'm fed up with it all.

But then, everyone is fed up with it all, all the time, epidemic or not. Doesn't everyone harbor a secret wish to be done with life, to have the peacefulness of death, oblivion?

I pick up the phone and dial Michael's number. Mama Jones answers, delighted that it is me calling. "Well, stranger, have you torn yourself away from the computer, or did it crash on you? We thought maybe you'd died . . . or something."

"How nice," I say, "that you're so welcoming and so polite. But no, I'm not dead. They're going to have to drive a stake through my heart to get rid of me. And speaking of riddance, how's Michael? Can I come by today and help out?"

"Not that much to help with, girl," Mama says. "But you're always welcome to bring that cute little bubble butt over."

"Fag hag," I tease.

"Come over after lunch. Michael says he wants to sit in the garden for a bit, which means getting him down two flights of stairs. You can help."

"Okay," I agree. "About half past one?"

"Yep," and Mama Jones hangs up.

I putter around my apartment, doing Saturday things — watering the plants, listening to Extra Fancy on the CD, and then X, rubbing oil into the woodwork, burning incense, and, as it is uncharacteristically warm out, throwing open all the windows. I fix myself lunch, some soup and a sandwich and then jump in the shower.

When I get to Michael's flat, I see Charlton's Mercedes parked in the driveway. Well, this will be a little party, I think as I ring the bell and Mama Jones buzzes me in. I find that Michael is already sitting in the garden, and he's looking rather pale in the dazzling sunlight. Charlton is smoking a cigarette as Michael chats with him.

Charlton looks up as I descend the back stairs. "Well look who's here," he says, waving a hand at the little redwood bench next to Michael. "We were just talking about you."

"Oh?" I say.

"Charlton was telling me about your consultation with Emma Kiljoy," Michael says. "You didn't tell me you needed therapy."

"Isn't it obvious?" I say.

"Yes, I suppose it is . . ." Michael's voice trails off. I can't tell if his remark is serious or a playful jab.

"*Very* obvious, I'd say," Charlton observes.

"Thank you both for your support," I say. "So, Michael, just how *are* you? You're looking better, I think." (In fact, I think Michael looks just terrible, wan and weak. But of course I don't say this.)

"Oh, up and down. Mostly down lately," Michael answers. "And how are you, my long-lost friend?"

"I'm fine—"

"That's why you're in therapy?" Michael asks.

"Oh . . . that . . . well, I just need to work a few things out. That's all. No big deal, really."

"Like what things?" Michael asks.

"Oh, you know, the usual," I say. "Midlife crisis, unprocessed grief, nightmares, hideous depression, suicidal fantasies, aging, looks, body issues. That's all."

"Good God!" Michael says. "That's rather a plateful, isn't it?"

"Well," Charlton says, drawing smoke into his lungs, "as a woman ages, she needs to do a little extra."

"Come on, guys," I say. "This isn't helping. The fact is, as good friends as you are, I'm embarrassed by my problems right now. It's all come tumbling down on my shoulders in the last couple of months . . . or years, maybe."

"I guess one of the advantages of dying," Michael says, "is that there's so much I don't have to worry about anymore."

"Don't talk like that," I say, and then regret it. Who am I to deny that Michael is, indeed, dying?

"I'll talk about anything I want," Michael says, annoyed.

"Anything, and at great length," Charlton says. "This girl will talk till she's blue in the face and we're all passed out from boredom—"

"Fuck you," Michael says.

"Isn't this pleasant?" I say. "Just a friendly little Saturday afternoon chat in the garden. When is Mama going to bring the tea and crumpets down?"

"Mama's not been feeling very well," Michael says. "She's been dragging her ass for the last month or so, and she complains that she has no energy. I worry about her."

"Oh, I think Mama is indestructible," Charlton says. "And I won't tell her that secretly, Michael refers to her as 'Mammy.'"

"Good God," I say. "You can't get any more racist than that," I say.

Michael is chuckling wickedly. "I'm dying, what do I care?"

"Still, it isn't right," I say.

We are all silent for a moment, then Charlton asks, "How are Scotty and Kent?"

"Oh, they're fine, just fine," I say. Scotty is my best friend, Kent is his boyfriend, and both of them are my housemates. Scotty, at twenty-nine, and Kent, at twenty-seven, have been lovers for three years. "There has been some tension lately, though, between them, because Kent wants to be more monogamous than Scotty wants, but you know Scotty . . . he's not about to give up the peep show and glory holes, or the midnight adventuring. He likens it to some sort of male hunting instinct. Oddly, Kent says he has no such instinct. He says he prefers to stick with one partner."

"Is this about jealousy? Or fear of loss? Or fear of infection?" Charlton asks.

"I think it's fear of infection," I say, "because Kent keeps bringing up the subject of safe sex, and he's told me that he worries about Scotty's midnight prowling, afraid that he'll slip up and find himself seroconverting."

Michael is frowning. "I forget what these young guys have to go through, worrying about getting infected. It's been such a given in my life that I've never had to deal with it that way. I just always assumed I had 'it,' and of course I did."

"It's not easy," I say, "because the expectation that people will be perfectly safe year after year, decade after decade, is just not realistic. 'Use a condom every time' suggests that perfection is possible, but it's not. Besides, condoms can break. Over a period of ten, fifteen, twenty years, something is bound to happen."

"You're saying it's a matter of when, not if," Charlton says. "I certainly don't know why I've stayed negative all through this. Lord knows there've been many close calls."

Michael has drifted off, his eyes closed. He looks very tired, and we offer to help him back upstairs. Together, Charlton and I take Michael between us and help him negotiate the wobbly back stairs to the flat, where Michael promptly collapses into bed.

Mad Mama Jones is making chocolate chip cookies, and she offers us some, fresh out of the oven, the chips still hot and gooey.

I study Mama Jones, thinking about Michael's comment that she hasn't been feeling well lately. She looks fine to me, as jolly and big-hearted as always. I decide not to say anything, not to ask her how she is.

3

As I walk to Dr. Kiljoy's office for my second therapy session, I pass the weasely little hippie boy who stands on the corner of Market and Sixteenth pleading with passersby to *please help me, I'm a good guy, help me out folks, help me get something to eat* . . .

He makes me ill. I just want to punch him in his sniveling mouth and tell him to get a job. After all, there's a help wanted sign in the cafe right where he stands on the corner. Compassion fatigue, again.

"How was your week?" Dr. Kiljoy asks, settling herself into her oversized leather chair.

"Nothing much," I say. "What do you want to know?"

"Well," she says, "how are you feeling?"

Ah, the feeling question. "About the same as always," I say. "Out of sorts, cross, confused. Certainly down in the dumps. I went to visit Michael — my sick friend, you remember? — and he was looking so bad that I thought I was going to have a panic attack. Of course, I told him he looked great, but in fact he's paler and thinner than ever. It got to me."

"Of course," she says. "You're having a hard time with his illness, aren't you?"

Silly woman. "Of course I'm having a hard time. Much of the time, I don't feel anything at all, and then I feel tired of it all, sometimes angry that it keeps on happening, even though the new meds are supposed to be such miracle cures."

"Well, I wouldn't say 'miracle cures' exactly," she says. "But many people have benefited enormously. I take it that Michael doesn't respond well?"

"No, no, not at all," I say. "In fact, it's worse than that. Last year he had a few good months on the new drugs, but by winter he was ghastly sick — yellow with liver failure, panting from pancreatitis. By the time we got him to the hospital, his kidneys had failed. So we were certain to lose him then."

"What happened?" she asks.

"Somehow he pulled through. For days and days he was on the edge. They were pumping him full of morphine and antibiotics and saline solution and god-knows-what else, and during the second week in the hospital, he just started getting better. His housemate — we call her Mad Mama Jones — moved in then to help take care of him. She lives rent-free in exchange for home nursing assistance.

"Under her care, Michael recovered, but he slowly started downhill this year. And he can't take another medication. When they tried a different one, his liver started acting up almost at once . . ." I let my voice trail off. I don't want to talk about this. Michael's illness is not why I came to therapy. And at these rates, I can't waste time just filling her in.

"What is it?" she asks, noting my silence.

"Oh, it's just . . . just that I . . . don't really want to talk about Michael or about the fucking epidemic. Not now, not anymore. I can't take any more of this shit."

She nods. "What would you like to talk about?"

"Don't you need more background info or something? Don't you want to know how my childhood was?"

She smiles. "How was your childhood?"

"Horrible," I say. "A typical American family — incest, molestation, weird disciplinary games, physical abuse, emotional abuse, church, church, and more church. My folks must have been making up for some kind of guilty conscience for all the church we went to . . . Sunday morning, Sunday evening, Wednesday night, Friday night, sometimes a trip to Los Angeles to attend a gospel concert or go to a revival."

"Yes, it does sound typical," she agrees. "But I don't think you really want to talk about this, either. What's on your mind today? How are you feeling right now?"

"Right now?" I echo her. "I feel worried that maybe I'm wasting my time and money sitting here. I feel preoccupied with the same damn things that have been bothering me for months — How do I look? How did I get these extra fifteen pounds? When am I finally going to get the results I want from the gym — and I've been going for a while now. Why am I so tired and depressed all the time? Why do I have to get older? Why do gay men value only physical beauty and sexual prowess? What am I going to do as I get even older?

"I tell myself, You should be happy, you have a nice apartment, great housemates, interesting work, a good car, enough money to be comfortable, and relatively good health. But instead of being happy, I feel miserable. Why do I have no sense of appreciation for the things I do have? I ought to be enjoying all of this, having the time of my life. But instead, I'm preoccupied — even obsessed — with what I see as a horrible decline in the quality of my life.

"My body is changing, broadening somehow, and . . . I guess I can say it . . . getting a little fat. I'm starting to lose my hair, which is why I shaved it all off. Of course, I do like the shaved-head look, so that's okay.

"I miss my old friends. I miss my lovers. I miss free time. I miss being young, I mean, really young, in my twenties. None of these things were problems back then. I just had a good time and everything worked out . . .

"I was poor, though, come to think of it, and I never knew what I thought about anything, and I couldn't hold my own in an argument . . .

"But why is my body betraying me? Why were my thirties just fine, but when I'm staring forty in the face, everything is starting to fall apart. Why?"

"It's aging," she says.

Please, give me a break, I think. Aging? At thirty-nine? I don't say anything for a few moments, and then:

"I guess I'm just confused, terribly confused. I don't know what to do next. It used to be that if you were HIV positive, you knew that you were just going to spiral downward into sickness and death. Now, with these new medications, that isn't even certain anymore. But it is for some people. How can you know which kind you are? How can you plan for the future?"

Pausing, I wait for Dr. Kiljoy to say something, but she just sits there, looking at me and making her little notes. I have the impression that she is looking *through* me as she thinks about something completely unrelated to what I'm saying.

I go on: "Everything in my life is coming up for review. I'm satisfied with nothing. It feels like everything needs to be changed, but when I try to think of what, specifically, to change, I draw blanks. Am I making any sense?"

"Yes, quite a bit, actually," she says.

I'm relieved. I thought she wasn't listening to me anymore, just sitting there thinking *What a bum, how boring, doesn't he know that everyone feels like that, and it only gets worse as you get older?*

But she has been listening after all.

A nervous silence fills the space between us. I am getting tired of repeating myself, or, at least, of feeling like I am repeating myself. The way my mind works, I just hash and re-hash the same damn thoughts, over and over. Redundancy.

"Sometimes I wonder if I ought to just move somewhere else, anywhere else, and get fat and spend my time just going to work and watching TV every evening. Then it wouldn't matter whether I looked old or young, fat or thin, or had the face of a god, or had the perfect gym-toned body.

"Gym-toned! How I hate that phrase! When I read through the personals columns in the papers, everyone describes themselves as 'gym-toned' or 'height/weight proportional.' What the hell does that tell you?

"And it doesn't help that I live with boys in their late twenties, because it just reminds me of what I've lost. It's like an open wound . . . oh, save me from these clichés!"

She smiles a thin, almost imperceptible smile. "Tell me about your housemates," she suggests.

"Well, there's two of them, Scotty and Kent. I met Scotty about six years ago, when he was twenty-two. He was working as a 'masseur' and 'model' and I called him to get together for a paid encounter. Well, he was so fucking cute that I got all hung up on him, spent way too much money on it, and then we parted ways after personal conflicts started to come up — things like me wanting too much from him, wanting romance and a relationship that he wasn't interested in, and he didn't seem capable of emotional intimacy. I even believed that it wasn't so much that he wasn't interested in me as much as it was that he was incapable of being interested in anyone, at least in a deep, intimate way.

"Maybe that was just self-delusion, to make his rejection more palatable to myself.

"After a while, though, the silent phone and the missing part of my life just ached too much, and we started to talk again, on the phone, forging a new relationship, a friendship really. We started to go to movies and stuff together, just usual friend stuff. He's now one of my closest friends.

"When he had a room open up in his huge flat — where he was living on Collingwood Street — we decided to try out being housemates. To make a long story even longer, we got along fine and began to set the place up as a real home, real family life — shared groceries, shared cooking and all that.

"Then he started dating Kent, who's very very cute and very very sexy. Eventually Kent moved in, too, and, basically, joined our little family. It's a pretty good setup, because we're all very close — physically intimate, but not sex, though we take naps together, trade massages, and blah blah blah. It's a really sweet relationship."

"And the sexual connection, this is over?" she asks.

"Yes, it's in the past," I answer. "From time to time, I feel like being sexual with Scotty, and sometimes with Kent, too, but I guess they just don't feel that way about me, so nothing ever happens.

"But with Scotty, it's not really about having sex. It would be more about making love. Our relationship is staggeringly deep. He's the first person I've ever grown to love so much that I want to make love to him just to express something that words don't seem adequate for . . . I've found it to be a rather sweet, tender feeling to want to love someone physically . . . and not be allowed, or able to. It's sort of a private, secret love. I like that."

"So, you have at least one primary relationship in your life," she says. "And yet you feel alone, confused, unattractive, and unlovable. Isn't there a contradiction there?"

I shift uncomfortably in my chair. "Yes, I suppose there is," I say. "But it's such a basic part of my nature that I don't really think of it, not until someone points it out like you just did."

"What do you mean that it's a basic part of your nature?" she asks.

I say, "Well, I've always been slow to feel things. I often don't feel anything at all, other than annoyance and depression, and self-pity and worry . . . what I'm trying to say is that I rarely actually *feel* loved, or cared about, even when I can see, plainly enough, and appreciate, intellectually, that love is present in my life. But I can't *feel* it. Not really, or only rarely. Once in a great while."

"And when you do actually feel cared about, how is that for you?" she asks.

"Painful," I say, and she nods. "It's too overwhelming when I do feel it, I usually dissolve in tears . . ."

I stop talking.

"What is it?" she prompts.

"Well, that's part of why I've come to talk with you, because I manage, somehow, always to turn even positive things into pain, into a strange sort of melancholy, a kind of yearning for something lost or never had. I think the strongest feeling I have — besides depression — is longing . . ."

"And? . . ."

"And I'm tired of it. I just want to be normal, I want to be un-depressed. I want things to be the simple way they were when I was younger."

"But you just told me that you felt dissatisfied for most of your life. Are you saying now that you were content when you were younger?"

"Not exactly content, I guess not . . . I mean, I *have* always felt excluded and uncared for. I *have* always felt the longing. But when I was younger, it was less disturbing to me, because I thought that things would happen in my life that would resolve that dissatisfaction, that would fill the loneliness.

"But that's not what's happened. What's happened is that the feeling of longing has intensified, and the feeling of discontentment is still churning, now taking on the form of unhappiness with myself in my body, at my age.

"It feels like it's the story of my life, this wanting or needing something, but I never know exactly what it is . . . I have enough years under my belt to know that materiality is not what I want. A new car or new clothes can make me feel good for a while, but they don't really do anything to fix this deeper yearning."

I stop talking, tired of hearing myself. These thoughts, these problems, have been with me as long as I can remember. I know that revisiting them will prove fruitless. But what, then, am I doing in therapy? Why am I sitting here blathering away?

Dr. Kiljoy sits still, looking pensive.

"Oh, I'm probably going on way too much. You need to know more about me, don't you? I mean, I'm going too deep right off the bat, aren't I?"

She smiles. "This is your hour, each week. You may talk about anything you like, in as much depth as you wish. If I need clarification, I'll let you know. Please go on."

I feel I can't talk anymore, at least not about all this heavy, troubled stuff. I have to change the subject. We talk for a few minutes about a piece of art on her wall, an Eidenberger etching of the Salzburg River in Austria. She told me that her family was originally from Salzburg, confirming what Charlton had told me about her background.

When the session is nearly over, I remember: "Oh, I almost forgot to tell you," I say, "I have a date to meet Anson — you know, my online buddy — this Friday evening. We're going to meet for dinner, and so the moment of truth is fast approaching."

"And how do you feel about that?" she says.

Is this some standard question, or what? "Well," I say, "I'm nervous, but I think that's natural enough. I have lots of hope, yet I don't want to be too eager, too desperate. But it would be nice to have a little romance in my life again. I'm not looking for marriage or monogamy, but romance is great, as long as it's not too gushy."

She smiles. "Gushy," she echoes. "Yes, it will be interesting to see how this date goes. I wish you well."

A little bit formal, this response, but time is up. It's time to leave.

Why do I feel as if the school bell has just rung and I'm being set free of a classroom?

◆

A mild heat wave has hung over the City for two days — blinding sunshine, smog ringing the horizon, air dirty and chokingly unbreathable, full of dust and pollen. People are either incredibly lethargic or super charged. Everyone is cranky. But there have been hints that the fog — the "marine layer" as one TV forecaster calls it (he must be from L.A.) — might roll in by late afternoon. I pray that this prophecy of impending fog will be fulfilled.

And as I leave Dr. Kiljoy's office and descend the stairs to the street, I turn to look up at Twin Peaks, ecstatic to see Sutro Tower swaddled in blessedly soft grey roiling fog. The air is sweet and cooling, as it should be, and the whisper of a chill lightens my step as I climb the steep hill of Collingwood Street.

4

I wake slowly. I don't know where I am. Not the room, not the apartment, not the city. I glance at the clock. Half past five in the morning. Slowly, groggily, the facts of my life come to me — my bedroom in San Francisco. I'm an editor. I read voraciously. I spend too much money on books. I live with two housemates, who have their own bedroom in this enormous flat. Who are obviously still asleep, as I hear nothing.

I grab the remote control and flip on the TV. Searching for the Weather Channel I stop at CNN, but there's nothing of any interest, no overnight disasters. The Weather Channel gives the San Francisco report: foggy, fifty-three degrees.

Taking the book from the bedside table — this week it's White's biography of Genet — I plump up the pillows and turn on the reading light.

But I can't concentrate on the book. Thoughts of Anson and our planned date intrude. Finally I give in, close the book, and lay there thinking, immersing myself in romantic fantasy

— will I find him attractive? Will he find me attractive? Will there be that spark of chemistry between us, as, indeed, our online communication suggests? Is he looking for a relationship, a real relationship?

Then, of course, the uncertainties: What if he doesn't find me attractive? What if he wants more than I do, marriage, monogamy, the whole nine yards? I've tried that before, and it was fine at the time, but I like more freedom than most people. What if I like him but he doesn't like me? Or vice versa? What if sex with him is really boring? What if he has a little dick?

My excitement, coupled with my apprehensions, create a delicious tension. Some might call this feeling excitement. I feel it as worry, or something akin to it. Curiosity? Idle speculation? A disaster in the making?

The alarm goes off again. My ten minutes of extra snoozing are over. I have to get up, shave my head, shower, get breakfast, read the world's worst newspaper — *The San Francisco Chronicle* — and get to work. Where I have far too much to do, five manuscripts piled on my desk. At least that will distract me from my daydreaming worries about Anson.

Neither of us has spoken online or sent e-mail to the other since we made the date. Of course what we're doing is letting the suspense build, drawing out the expectant mood before we meet. Luscious expectation.

Work is too busy, as usual. An office meeting, an editorial meeting, and a dreadful lunch with a terrible New Age writer (who, despite her lack of talent as a writer, has an enormous international following of devotees devoted to channeling and various forms of clairvoyance) — all these conspire to make it impossible for me to forge ahead on any of the manuscripts piled on my desk.

Late in the afternoon, I take a call from Michael:

"Hey, how's it going?" I ask.

"Not so good," he says. I roll my eyes, glad that he can't see my expression. Just once, it would be nice to hear him say that he's feeling good. But his illness (advanced as it is), coupled with his depression (as indulgent as it is), added to his miserable finances (poor as they are) all render his life nothing less than gruesome. I, of course, say nothing like this.

"What's the matter?" I ask.

"Well, I've got a terrific, brain-splitting headache, which makes me wonder if I'm coming down with meningitis—"

"Do you have a stiff neck?" I interrupt. (We have all become superb diagnosticians these days.)

"No, no stiff neck," he says. "But I am running a slight fever, around a hundred or so."

What else is new? I think, but don't say. "Oh, that's rotten, fevers always make you so listless."

"That's a good word," Michael says. "That's exactly how I feel. Of course my depression is worse, because I can't get out to the garden today, not with this fever and headache."

I say (unbelieving myself): "Well, I'm sure it's nothing but a fever and a headache. Nothing more." Which is patently absurd. Anyone with late-stage AIDS does not have "just" a fever or headache. It's always something dreadful. Or at least fear-making.

"But there's more . . ." His voice trails off.

"What else?" I ask.

"Well, this bad toe of mine — you know the one with the fungal infection—"

"I thought they all were infected," I cut in.

"Well, they are, but this is the really bad one, the big toe on my left foot."

"Yes?"

"It's turning purple."

"Oh," I say, brilliantly. "What does your doctor think of that?"

"I haven't talked to him since the week before last," Michael answers. "Do you think I should?"

"If your toe is turning purple, it might be worth a call to the doctor."

"Okay, I guess you're right . . . I'm sorry to bother you at work like this, but I always—"

"No, it's fine, but I do have to go," I say. "But I'll call you later."

"Okay, fine. Thank you," Michael says, hanging up.

This is the weekly ritual with Michael. I grow so bored with his litany of medical complaints that I become utterly exasperated. But, I remind myself, this is what Michael's life is about. Illness. Impending death. All the little (and big) aches and pains and worries and concerns and obsessions about health. There's very little else left to him. This is why I, and everyone else, indulge him. But God, I get tired of it.

I'll have to talk this over with Dr. Kiljoy, I think. And then realize: there's nothing to talk about. It's very simple — Michael is sick, and caregiving is a rotten chore. Nothing more, nothing less.

But this nonchalant (accepting?) attitude never fully satisfies me. Because gnawing at the back of my mind is the freakiness of it all. This entire epidemic, these countless losses, these horrors and tortures — is this normal life? How can we go on, without losing what little grip on reality we might have?

I do not pursue this thought. I have been there before. It goes nowhere but down.

At the end of the workday, I heave a sigh and trudge onto MUNI, surely the world's slowest and most inefficient transit system (it is so bad, I expect to see peasants on board, with chickens and twelve kids in tow). We passengers sit and stand there in absolute silence, the only sound the roar of the train through the underground tunnels.

I glance up (I have been lucky enough to get a seat, elbowing two Chinese ladies and three teenage hooligans out of the way) and notice a young man — boy almost — who is staring at me. Or is staring at the top of my head, it seems. He smiles. I smile. He reaches down and adjusts himself, allowing, for a moment, a clear view of his large (and tempting) equipment pressed against his khaki pants. He smiles again. I smile again. The train drags into Castro Station, and he is gone.

I love these little gifts from the universe, I think. Tantalizing moments of highly-charged, lowdown lewdness. I step from the station feeling that life is, indeed, worth living.

Perhaps, after all, I'm going to find that things are improving. Perhaps, with therapy, and with a boyfriend — Anson, though this is jumping the gun — the loneliness and darkness will recede a little bit. Perhaps there is a solution to this gloom, this mid-life crisis, this lingering, baneful dismay at what life has become.

Later, puttering around the apartment, I am thinking about my date with Anson. He sent me e-mail today: *Just confirming our dinner date for tomorrow night. To tell you the truth, I'm excited and scared. But let's see how it goes. Can't wait!*

Life can be so enticing. And so nerve-wracking. Why must people date? Why can't we all have arranged marriages or something like that? Where we wouldn't have to endure the agonizing ritual of dating, getting to know someone, and all that bother? Once one finds oneself in a relationship — be it romantic or friendly or even family — it can be so enriching and so darned comfortable that one wonders why one cannot simply skip the first part and go directly to the comfortable part. It would be much, much easier. And think of the money that would be saved!

I laugh at my own silliness. If it were possible to skip ahead to the comfortable part, then we'd lose the intriguing, exciting part, the mystery of it all, and thus, the romance of it all. That scrumptious not-knowingness.

Charlton calls, wanting to go to lunch the next day. I accept, knowing that a good lunch with him will ease my tension about dinner with Anson.

Charlton meets me at the Hayes Street Grill. As always, I order swordfish and white wine. Charlton orders a Bloody Mary and salmon. We eye the waiter with embarrassing lust. "Look at that!" Charlton declares. He doesn't have to define "it." I know he means the waiter's butt, very cute, very round, and very firm. "My god, it has a life of its own," I agree.

"You know, you ought to be a little more daring and try something else on the menu," Charlton says.

"But I like swordfish, I love swordfish," I say. "Why should I order something else?"

"Just for the sake of variety," Charlton says. "The way you like your men. Never the same one twice."

"Tired old queen," I say. "And bitter, too."

Charlton laughs. "Speaking of tired, bitter, and old, how's your therapy coming along?"

"Oh, you!" I say. Then go on, "I guess it's coming along okay. I'm still not really sure what it is that's bugging me, but I am a little more confident that there is something I can work out that will give me some peace of mind. I mean, I'm going to be forty, and I'm still worried about my waist size, about how big or not my muscles are, whether or not my dick is big enough, how come I don't look like those boys at the gym—"

"The buff boys," Charlton cuts in.

"Yes, them," I say. "It's like I anticipate that my life is about to crumble around me, because I'm not going to be in my thirties anymore."

"Well, as someone who hasn't seen their thirties in a little bit of time—"

"Little bit?" I say, sarcastically.

"Excuse me, but I'm trying to tell you something of great value, impart some worldly wisdom to your approaching midlife crisis—"

"Oh, yes, that . . ." I say.

"Well, yes," Charlton goes on. "As someone with a bit more time in this life than you, let me say that it only gets worse."

I let out a breath. "Gee, thanks so much. That really helps."

"I thought it might," he says. "My pleasure."

The waiter arrives with my glass of wine and Charlton's Bloody Mary. We toast youth and drink greedily.

"Speaking of youth," Charlton says, "How are Scotty and Kent these days?"

"Oh, about the same," I answer, "which is to say that there've been no new dramas. They have been quarreling, of course, but that goes without saying. It's the same old stuff."

"The monogamy thing?" Charlton asks.

"Yeah, that's it. Kent throws a hissy fit about once a month, gets his knickers in a twist about Scotty's visits to the peep show, the glory holes, Blow Buddies, and wherever else he goes. But Kent, of course, thinks it's too risky. Or so he says."

"I'd guess what it comes down to," Charlton observes, "is that Kent wants to play around with Scotty without condoms. That's the only thing that makes any sense here."

"I'm sure that's part of it," I agree, "but Kent says that he's just not comfortable with an open relationship. He says that it makes him crazy to think about Scotty having sex with other people."

"Then don't think about it," Charlton says, sarcastically.

"Exactly," I say. "But Kent is unenlightened on this topic. He's never had an open relationship before, and he's way, way codependent. Feels that he should own Scotty or something, at least should be able to control his behavior."

The waiter brings our salads. "How distasteful," Charlton observes.

The waiter hesitates. "Is something wrong, sir?" he asks.

"Oh, no!" Charlton says. "I was commenting on something my friend just said. No, no, the salad is fine."

The waiter withdraws, a sneer on his face nonetheless. One of those waiters who believe they are the son of God.

"Of course Kent doesn't realize he's being a codependent mess—"

"Or asshole, to put it another way."

"Yes," I agree, "because Kent has never had any exposure to recovery or therapy or anything else along those lines. When I've tried to talk to him about it, he just yawns and grows defensive, saying something along the lines of This Is Normal, Promiscuity Should Be Over, etcetera, etcetera."

"How old is he?" Charlton asks.

"Twenty-seven," I say.

"Ah," Charlton intones. "That means he came of age during the Reagan years and bought the whole Nancy Reagan right-wing nonsense wholesale. 'Just Say No' and all that. I find it amazing that kids, especially queer ones, could swallow that garbage, that sex is bad, abstinence is possible — even healthy! — and that we should all be cowering under the leadership of the Moral Majority or whatever it's called these days."

"I agree," I say. "I try to tell him this, try to help him see that he needs to develop his own rules, not accept what is being crammed down his throat, but he won't see it."

"Or can't," Charlton says. "And speaking of cramming down throats, do you see that one who's being seated over there in the corner?"

I glance in the direction of Charlton's gaze. "Oh, yes, I do see," I say.

"Very well built," he says.

"In every way," I agree.

We finish our salads. Charlton orders another Bloody Mary. I order another glass of wine. The waiter brings the drinks, and then the food. My steaming swordfish looks scrumptious.

"Any word from Michael?" Charlton asks.

"Just the usual weekly call. He says his big toe is turning purple."

"Purple?" Charlton asks.

"Yes, I told him to call the doctor. And he was imagining that he was coming down with spinal meningitis—"

"Did he have a stiff neck?" Charlton interjects.

"No, he didn't. I told him not to worry . . . but of course, that's not really the right advice, is it? How can he not worry?"

"Exactly," Charlton says

"Well, I wish that Scotty and Kent would iron out their differences," Charlton says. "It seems a shame — two gorgeous boys in their twenties, living together, with good jobs, enough money to get a good start on life. They should be happy, having the time of their lives. Not bickering over silly issues like faithfulness and promiscuity. God, what an ancient word, archaic, really."

"I agree," I say. "I can always tell when they're quarreling about it again, because Kent lays in bed staring at the TV, and Scotty is out, nowhere to be found. Of course he's at the peep show blowing off the steam that Kent arouses through his absurd demands. It's those times that I wish I lived alone again."

"Oh, but then you couldn't afford that fancy car of yours," Charlton says.

We eat in silence for several minutes, savoring the wonderful food. As Charlton finishes his plate, he says, "You haven't told me much about your sessions with Dr. Kiljoy."

"Not much to tell, yet, really. We've only had two sessions. So I don't feel any different. Well, perhaps I feel more confused, because I'm not altogether sure why I'm in therapy."

"Because you're a depressed, fucked-up mess," Charlton says. "You need help."

"Thanks," I say. "I can always count on you."

After lunch, I can't concentrate, so I leave work early and go sit at Cafe Flore and drink coffee. They are playing Chet Baker, the perfect choice for a lazy summer afternoon. Two lesbians sit beside me, their hair three colors each, piercings in their noses, eyebrows, ears, and lips. They are arguing. The heavyset one says, emphatically, "But I thought you were more politically motivated than that!" And the other replies, heatedly, "Politics, schmolitics, I'm sick of your egocentric feminism." They shut up and glare at each other.

Across the room, and through the window, I see a cute shaved head boy, his brow furrowed as he studies a large book open before him. Another boy, strangely buffed for the Flore, sits beside him and smiles, trying to win the boy's attention. He is ignored.

I stand outside the no-name restaurant on Market Street, awaiting Anson's arrival. Wind sweeps down from Twin Peaks, where roiling fog swirls around the base of Sutro Tower. I shudder and wonder if I should step into the restaurant's bar, wait there. But I don't want Anson to have to come looking for me. That would be uncomfortable for him, possibly. He might think that I'm a no-show if he doesn't find me waiting here.

Another gust of wind slaps me, and in the distance, up Market Street, I catch a flash of shaved head, and I know it's him. Even though there's a shaved head behind every tree in San Francisco these days, I know it's him. And he's cute. Very cute. Cuter than I would have imagined. He's wearing all black (of course, as am I) and he is walking with a purpose, not strolling. He sees me eyeing him and smiles, knowing that I am *his* date.

He reaches me and we both smile, nerves taking hold instantly. I fumble to offer my hand, laughing, saying Well, hello. He shakes my proffered hand and says, And I'm Anson. Great to meet you. We exchange the usual first-time pleasantries, and for once, I'm happy that there are manners to cover over the uneasiness of meeting someone new.

"Let's go in," I say, as more icy wind slams us. We enter the restaurant, the hostess seats us, we order drinks — ice tea for me and sparkling water for him — and settle in for a few silent, tense moments.

"This is silly," I say, "but I'm nervous. I know I shouldn't be, because we've talked so much over the computer, but . . ."

He shrugs his shoulders and smiles. "Thank god you said it. No, we shouldn't be nervous, but of course we are. Don't you just hate this part of dating? Meeting someone for the first time, wanting to make a good impression, scared out of your wits that he's going to think you're ugly or something?"

"But you're not ugly," I say, already the flirt. "Not at all."

"And I could return the compliment," he says. I think I blush, but it may just be my blood pressure.

"You're blushing . . . already," he says. And we both laugh, easing the strain.

"I do know what you mean," I say. "I've had too many dates where the first thing you think when you meet the guy is Oh, no, how am I going to get through this?"

He smiles warmly. "Exactly, and you're wondering how you can diplomatically hurry the evening along, just so you can get it over with."

"You know," I say, "I've actually gotten pretty good about saying right away — if it doesn't feel right, or if I'm not attracted — that it isn't going to work for me. That way, the date is over, and you've spared yourself — and him — the agony of completing a date that neither of you wants to be on."

"Unless he doesn't feel the same way," he says. "Then you know you're going to hurt their feelings."

"It's true," I say. "And there are far too many hurt feelings in the world as it is."

He gives me a curious look, as though he admires this frankness. I take a deep breath and unfold my napkin, lay it in my lap. He does the same. The waiter, a tall, thin boy with about twenty facial piercings, brings our drinks and asks if we've decided.

"Oh, we haven't looked at the menu yet," Anson says. "Give us a minute."

The waiter steps away. "Well, there you go. You know we won't see him for another half hour. They *never* come back when you tell them you're not ready yet."

"Well, then, he'll just be cutting into his tip, won't he?"

I raise my eyebrows. "Catty, catty . . . I guess I forgot your caustic nature, though you've displayed it often enough online!"

He smiles, staring down at the menu. "I think the chicken sounds good—"

"Oh, I was looking at the chipotle pork tacos," I say. "I wonder how spicy they are?"

Miraculously, the waiter reappears to take our order. After querying him about the tacos, I order them, and Anson orders the fish. We sip our drinks and are quiet for a moment. "You know," he says softly, "I feel that I already know you, we've talked so much on the computer. It's almost like meeting an old friend, rather than going on a new date for the first time."

I nod in agreement. He goes on in this vein, mentioning previous "conversations" we've had, laughing about other users we mutually know. For a long moment, I look directly into his eyes, those cool blue eyes, and for the briefest flash I see us together, really together. Such intuition has only fallen over me three other times in my life — with the three men who became my lovers. I know, somehow, that this is the real thing (as they say), that Anson and I will have a relationship with staying power.

I ask him how his classes are going (he's studying at UCSF to be a pharmacist). Fine, he says, and then the waiter brings our food. We savor the first bites, declaring how good it all is. (I wonder how good it actually is, because this restaurant is not all that great, just convenient; is my mood of hopeful romanticism making everything seem superbly tasty?)

"Once, when we were online, you mentioned that you had a relationship with Scotty, your housemate," Anson says. It's not just an observation. It's a question.

"Oh, yes, I did," I answer, "I mean I do . . . I mean I did say that I do have a relationship with Scotty." It occurs to me that of course he wants to know more. He can't know what I mean by using the word relationship; he probably assumes I mean lover.

Anson takes another bite of his chicken and looks at me, expectantly. I ponder how to explain it all. Then forge ahead: "Scotty and I used to have sex, many years ago. He was a call boy, and I went head over heels for him. But he wasn't interested in being boyfriends, or lovers. But he was interested in having a relationship that was more than friends, more than best friends really."

I pause, sipping my ice tea. "After many rocky years, we finally reached an arrangement that has proven to be quite wonderful. But it's hard to explain, because our society, even gay society, doesn't have words to describe this sort of relationship. Scotty and I are very, very close, physically intimate — not sexual, though — like taking naps together, sleeping together occasionally, snuggling up, trading massages, that sort of thing.

"We share our household like an old married couple, and with Scotty's boyfriend Kent, who also lives with us, it's one of those chosen, fought-for, gay families that we're always talking about."

Anson is nodding his head yes. (Is that relief I see in his eyes? Does he suddenly feel that yes, the door is open for us after all?)

"It's pretty common, I think, among queers, to have a pair of partners . . . or whatever the word should be . . . that are extraordinarily close, though not sexually linked as in lovers or boyfriends, but who are committed to making a home and life together. That's what we have."

"But what does Scotty's boyfriend think of all this?" Anson asks. A good question. One that I never truly know the answer to.

"Well, he seems fine with it," I answer. "But I'm never sure that he fully understands what it means to have the sort of relationship that Scotty and I have. But we get along well enough, though Kent is prone to throw tantrums on a somewhat regular basis.

"The bottom line is—" I stop myself, dismayed that I have just used a phrase I find abhorring. "The thing is, what I don't have in my life, and what I want, is romance, a boyfriend, lover, whatever you want to call it . . ."

Anson is quiet for a moment, taking this all in. I am suddenly embarrassed, fearing that I have divulged too much, made myself too vulnerable

"That's good to know," Anson says, and my apprehensions are relieved. We *are* on the same wave length.

When it comes time to leave, there is the awkward moment outside the restaurant, when neither of us knows what to do or say next. I take the plunge:

"Come to my place," I say. And Anson says yes, he'd like that. We walk through the Castro, saying very little, the tension of excitement between us like a tender thread that neither of us wants to break by saying the wrong thing, or making the wrong move.

"My place is rather nice," I say, as I open the door (for I sometimes feel self-conscious about the abundance of mahogany antiques, the Persian and Navajo rugs, the gothic iron chandeliers. It is the home of a former goth gone into some money).

When I switch on the light, Anson lets out a low whistle. "If I were straight, I'd say 'awesome', but since I'm queer, I'll just say cool."

We walk through to my rooms, and by the time we get there, we are already pawing each other. Anson takes my face in his hands, looks me in the eye, and then brings his mouth to mine. I start melting. When he reaches under my shirt and lightly pinches my nipples, I am hard, ready, and enslaved. It has been ages since I've felt this sort of passion, years I think.

Anson is very gentle. He sits on the edge of the bed and reaches up to undo my pants. Pulling them down, my cock springs free and he leans to take it into his mouth. As he sucks, he wriggles out of his clothes, and I wrestle myself nude as well.

In the midst of our lovemaking, I feel many things: excitement (of course), longing, satisfaction, grief (for my dead lovers), affection, and hope. When Anson pulls me onto the bed, on top of him, I laugh. "What's so funny?" he asks. And I answer, "It's been a long time since I've had sex in bed. It's almost always standing, vertical intercourse."

He smiles, gives one soft laugh, and draws me tight against his body.

Afterwards, he curls up beside me and says, "This is when we're supposed to have a cigarette."

"But I don't smoke in the house," I say.

We lay entwined for a long time, completely silent. One thing that pleases me is that he's not one of those people who has to jump into the shower directly after sex, as if to wash away the evidence of sin or something. I enjoy being a little messy for a while, sweat drying on our chests, come forming little gelatinous mounds on our legs.

We fall asleep that way, unshowered, wound up in each other's arms and legs.

5

Over the hill beyond my window, I can see a hill topped by a rough outcropping of red rock; at the edge of the horizon, cottonball clouds drift eastward. The sea breeze is blowing, rather hard. Patches of cerulean skies are deep and rich, like clean, polished carnival glass. Waking, I feel refreshed, calm.

Scotty, Kent, and I attend a rock concert at the Warfield. Getting there is like hell to pay, circling, hunting, then finally parking, making our way through a sea of homeless, and kooks, and crack addicts, junkies, freaks, skatepunks. We arrive just as the Lunachicks take the stage. As usual, the sound is fucked up. The mixer is drunk, no doubt, or on dope. We shout The mixing sucks!, but he takes no heed. We stuff our ears with plugs of torn tissue, cutting out the deafening overtones. These people know nothing of music. Only noise. The Lunachicks are boring. The crowd drifts and chatters. A fog of cigarette smoke hangs over the pit. There is the pungent scent of marijuana. The pit is still, unmoving. The lead singer steps out of her spotlight, over and over again. Makes no sense.

Reverend Horton Heat comes up next, interesting enough, bland in sum. After four songs I say I am tired, and Scotty and Kent say Let's go. We leave. We push through the crowd. Green hair. Pink mohawks. Black leather, black cotton, black, black, black. Lovers of the gothic. I feel uncool in my green jeans and plaid pendleton, some sort of throwback to the grunge of the early nineties. I don't really care. Scotty stops in the lobby to register to vote. He declares, in the space allotted for party affiliation, "no party." I say Not a Democrat? He says no, independent. Hard for me to understand. I am a Jimmy Carter democrat, through and through. He laughs at me.

Outside the theater, half past ten, more human detritus to wade through. Like forging a battlefield of wounded soldiers. Spare a quarter? Some change? Weed? Smoke? Water? This begging and these offers of drugs bore me, disgust me.

❖

Dr. Kiljoy seats herself and smiles. "Have you had a good week?" she asks.

"Oh, pretty good, fair, I guess," I say. Then remain silent. She nods, prompting me to speak. "I'm never sure how to begin," I say. "It seems that when I get here, I feel fine, like there's nothing really on my mind, but that can't be true, because why else would I be here?"

Dr. Kiljoy smiles and nods again. "Why don't you begin by telling me what happened this week."

I sigh. I look towards the windows. A pale, milky light is pooling in the velvet drapes. Okay. "Well . . . I worked, I talked to Michael, went to a rock concert with Scotty and Kent, had lunch with Charlton — who says hello — I read three books, worked too hard, went to the gym. Oh, and I had my date with Anson."

"And how did that go?" she asks.

"It was actually quite wonderful," I say. "I hadn't understood just how hungry I was for romance until we went out. And it was very romantic, a nice dinner with dessert, good conversation, and a light-hearted, good feeling in general."

She smiles and nods her head. I go on, "But of course I was filled with self doubt, especially afterwards—"

"Why afterwards?" she asks.

"Because it was all so perfect. That made me question whether or not it was actually like that, or an illusion colored by my romantic longings. I've usually felt this way before, when dating someone who I intuitively knew might be a potential partner . . . in the long haul, I mean . . . I've wondered just what I'm getting myself into. Am I ready to have someone in my life again? Or am I finished with relationships, at least relationships of this kind? What will I do if it starts crowding me, starts cutting into my time so much that I feel trapped?"

"All common concerns," she says, reaching for her notepad. That damned notepad. I wish I knew what she was writing down.

"He asked me about my relationship with Scotty, and I explained that to him. But I'm not sure he understood it. I think he did. I hope. But I may have gone too far in describing the sort of romantic interaction I'm looking for—"

"You just said that perhaps you weren't looking for that kind of relationship," she observes.

"Hmm . . . well, yes . . . the thing is, I'm all over the map with it. And I'm not sure I'm going to figure it out in time to know how to make the next move."

She looks up from her notes. "The only thing to do next is what feels right at the time. Of course examining your feelings, and motives, and your thoughts is a good thing, because it will help direct you when you are making your next moves, but there's no way to foresee that. You must do what feels right to you, whatever you *want* to do."

I ponder this for a moment, remembering. "My uncle Karl used to say something along the same lines, about always following the path of least resistance—"

"That's it exactly," she says, almost triumphantly. I feel as if I have just passed some test.

"But I guess this isn't what I'm here to talk about, is it? I'm here to figure out what I'm going to do about aging, and losing my youth, and losing — or forfeiting — the quest for personal beauty. I want to know how to grow up."

There, I've said it. "Facing forty, I think it's not very becoming to act like a kid anymore, but I don't know how to be an adult, how to make the leap to the other side of what I see as a great divide. How can I do that?"

"We'll have to see," she says. Typical, I think. A hundred and fifty dollars an hour — no, fifty minutes — and she says wait and see. That really pisses me off.

I sit quietly for a few moments, letting my eyes rest on the far wall, filled from floor to ceiling with books. The pale, baneful light seeps through the long windows behind her desk. A table lamp — art deco — casts a warm haze across a highly polished mahogany table, on which a spray of yellow roses sits.

I keep my silence a moment longer, feeling resistant, rebellious (almost).

Dr. Kiljoy takes up her notepad and pen, smiles (almost imperceptibly), and asks: "In our first session, you stated that you had 'survived AA and NA.' Would you care to elaborate on your experiences in that realm?"

Oh, sweet Jesus, I think. Another fucking narrative about my fucked-up life. The part about booze and pills isn't very pretty, and I've had to revisit this personal history many, many times — in other therapies, in meetings, to my close friends, my co-workers. But I guess it's probably important for Kiljoy to know just how fucked up I can be.

"All my life I've been fucked up," I begin. I hesitate. Do I really want to go on about this? Should I just tell her that I really don't want to talk about it? But then, of course she needs to know me, know my past troubles, know the kinds of demons I struggle with. What the hell.

"I was raised in a very strict Baptist household, as I've told you before. My folks were so uptight about everything — smoking, dancing, makeup, drinking, sex — that all these things became extraordinarily tantalizing to me. I remember my fantasy in adolescence was to have my own apartment in Los Angeles, where I would go to UCLA and be free to drink, smoke, and watch horror movies. That was my idea of adulthood, of the perfect grown up life.

"And I think I got off to a good start, smoking at fourteen with the lowlife Mexican girls at the taco stand, learning curse words in Spanish. I had my first adult sexual experience at sixteen, a guy that taught me just about everything. When I went away to college I was able to embark on a life of real decadence — pot smoking, cocaine, cigarettes, and lots of booze, preferably Jim Beam.

"But I was always prone to panic attacks, even though I didn't know what they were. I just would get all short of breath and feel such horrible doom that I'd have to run out of the room and walk for miles and miles just to calm down.

"Later on, when I moved to San Francisco at twenty-five, after grad school, I heard about anxiety, and panic attacks, and I heard that the thing to do for them was to take tranquilizers. Thus began my twelve-year love affair with Valium, Ativan, Xanax, Librium, Seconal, Dalmane, Halcion . . . you name any downer, I've done it . . . Percodan, Dilaudid, Vicodin . . . the list goes on.

"Eventually I decided to stop all this pill popping, so the day my last lover died, I vowed never to take another pill or drink. I went through hell, but I — and everyone around me — just thought I was experiencing deep grief over the loss of my lover. What I was really going through was withdrawal from tranquilizers, one of the most horrible, if not the most horrible, experiences of my life. I'm surprised I didn't die from it, because people do, you know . . ."

Dr. Kiljoy nods in agreement. "So how did you find your way to Alcoholics Anonymous?" she asks.

"I was having a terrible time with the crush on Scotty. I'd just met him and was head over heels for him. A friend told me that I was obsessed, sick about it, and that I should go to a meeting of Codependents Anonymous. So I went, and my world started to change, dramatically.

"In the course of those meetings, I began to suspect that there was something wrong with me that had to do with 'substances' — because by this time I was taking tranquilizers and pain pills again, heavily — and then it all just hit me at once that I was addicted, that I was dependent on pills, and that I better get cleaned up.

"So I went to a Narcotics Anonymous meeting, held my hand up as a newcomer, and started on the road to recovery."

"And how long ago was that?" she asks.

"About six years ago. I have five years clean and sober. But it hasn't been easy, and a lot of the time I don't really feel that I even belong in those groups. I mostly just go to AA now. But sometimes I wonder if what I went through was just the usual trials and tribulations of youth."

"But you don't drink or use pills now?"

"No, not now, not really."

I stop talking. She's writing notes. Through the window, I see that the light is darkening, fog must be rolling in. Somewhere in the distance, someone is honking their horn, over and over.

"I don't think that any of this has much to do with my current situation," I (quietly) say.

"No, perhaps not," she says, "but it's all useful information for me. Tell me, when you stopped using everything, and began attending meetings, did you have a period of clarity, of a crumbling of memory?"

"Yes, yes, as a matter of fact," I say. "We call it the breakdown of denial. And it was a shocking revelation, to me, to see that what I had always envisioned as an idyllic childhood — you know, romping in the piles of autumn leaves, coming home from school to the aroma of chocolate chip cookies baking, an innocent time of ease and curiosity — was in actuality a mess of lies, bizarre punishments, delinquent behavior, like fire-starting, vandalism, shoplifting, and, even though it's practically a cliché in America, molestation."

I stop talking, annoyed that we are going into all this. This is water under the bridge. I want help in the here and now. I want to feel better, I want to know what's troubling me, why I can't take pleasure in anything anymore. But then, I think of Anson, and our romantic evening, and I tell myself that no, I'm not completely dead inside. There is a warm tingling in my body at the thought of that beautiful man.

I say: "Oh, but this is typical stuff, the usual nonsense of childhood in America. We don't really need to go into all this. I've given you a fair picture of things as it is."

She nods her head, (thankfully) in agreement. Good, I think, we don't have to waste more time and money on this ancient bullshit. Some of my annoyance dissipates, but I see that I'm tapping my foot repeatedly, nervously. I'm eager to be done with this session, to get out, go to Cafe Flore, have a cup of coffee, smoke a cigarette, and watch the fog blanket the Castro.

She senses my mounting irritability. "You seem a bit impatient, as though you feel you'd rather not be here."

"Um . . . well . . ." I stutter. "It's just that I don't need to go through all this stuff so long after the dust has settled. It's one of my pet peeves about therapy, that we spend so much time dwelling on the past, illuminating and revisiting and reviewing childhood and problems and circumstances that have long ceased to be relevant to my life today. It bothers me that therapy seems always to focus on problems, rather than solutions."

"Is that what you think is going on here?" she asks.

Sensing that she is bristling, I say, "Yes, somewhat. I didn't come here to rehash my rotten childhood, or my early adulthood. I came here because I'm about to turn forty and I feel like a failure. I'm cranky and cross all the time. I'm impatient with Michael, wishing he'd either get well or die. Scotty and Kent are quarreling again about monogamy. Everywhere I look in my life, it's doom and gloom and sadness and, most of all, inertia."

Have I upped the ante? Is she truly aroused by this blatant criticism of therapy? I go on, digging in, "Therapy seems to lack any notion of getting better. Maybe transformation would be a better word. How can I make things better if I'm spending my time examining everything that's wrong?"

She has taken on a sober expression, blank and seemingly cold. I am quiet, now feeling badly about my attack on her profession, and, indirectly, her.

She smiles slightly. "I'd like to refer you to a psychiatrist. I believe that you are depressed, in the clinical sense of the term, and I think that anti-depressant medication would likely help you feel much better."

Oh, god, Prozac here we come, I think. But my world is sufficiently gloomy enough that I don't argue with the idea. Maybe medication is a big step in the right direction. Lord knows, nearly everyone around me is on one anti-depressant or another.

"Okay," I say. "I'm willing to see a psychiatrist."

"Now this would only be for a consultation, for him to evaluate your mood and prescribe an appropriate anti-depressant. We, of course, will continue to meet weekly. Is that clear?"

What a patronizing tone, I think. "Yes, sure," I say, again vaguely annoyed.

She writes down the name and phone number of a Dr. Elliot Quackenbush. I promise to call him this afternoon.

6

The fog has cleared and a heat wave is upon us, simmering, sweat-making heat. "Hot as a pistol," my father used to say. This heat destroys motivation, slays the town. All is slow and dusty.

The air is motionless. Wild parrots cry in the palm trees down Market Street. I sweat. I pray. I wait for inspiration, not wanting to call anyone, not wanting to read or think or move. Work is done for the week. My legs hurt.

◆

More heat, one-hundred degrees in San Francisco. Rough time, sweating while just sitting down. Thick orange haze. Light milky. Oddly quiet: earthquake weather. Agonizing heat. Relentless sun.

I sit at Peet's and sip an iced coffee. I go home and listen to Nick Cave and the Bad Seeds. I listen to REM, X, White

Zombie. I long for my younger self, in that era of truly new music — the Plasmatics, Nina Hagen, Plastique Bertrand, the B52s, Men Without Hats. I remember my days in ACT UP, the bickering and in-fighting, the exhilaration of a protest, an action.

The heat wave continues, unrelenting. All day long, from half past five in the morning till eight at night, the sun burns across the city, creating a somber lethargy, a vague melancholy. I talk to my mother on the phone. In the Central Valley, where she now lives, it's one-hundred ten degrees. I recall my teen years, when we lived in the house east of San Diego, the house with the pool. My brothers and sisters and I would float on air mattresses all afternoon, frying our young skin, turning first bronze, then brown under that ceaseless, burning Southern California sun.

I turn on the computer and check for e-mail. Of course there's a message from Anson:

> *Just a note to let you know how much I enjoyed our dinner*
> *and finally getting to meet, at long last. You're great,*
> *I think, and I hope that we'll get together again soon.*
> *Oh, and by the way, the sex was great.*

My heart expands as I read this message. Hopeless romantic. Can one be a hopeless romantic and a cynic at the same time? I dash off a reply, saying that I, too, was thrilled, and yes, I thought the sex was great.

I see Dr. Quackenbush. He listens to my complaints for about five minutes and then reaches for his prescription pad. He thinks I'm a good candidate for Wellbutrin, so I leave the office, Rx in hand, and go directly to the pharmacy. My eagerness betrays my desperation. This gloom has got to lift. I'll try anything.

◆

The heat wave has broken and the fog is in, thick and dark, dripping. At night, drifting off to sleep, I hear the melancholy wail of foghorns on the Bay. I walk the streets these brooding days, reveling in the muted spirit of the City under grey skies, tasting the mist on my lips, watching the skies change from one shade of grey to another. I walk and walk, this Saturday, all the way from the Castro to Civic Center, past the Opera House, out Polk Street to the Marina and Fisherman's Wharf. I pause at the Wax Museum, thinking it might be fun. A crowd of fat white tourists rushes the ticket counter; I decide against it. I look across the waters to Alcatraz, its lonely searchlight strobing rhythmically. A massive steel freighter is making its way through the narrow channel of the Golden Gate.

I walk on to North Beach, stopping at the Savoy Tivoli for an espresso. I peruse the new titles at City Lights. I look up at the marquee of the club where Carol Doda used to exhibit her manufactured bosom. I walk back through Chinatown, recalling my childhood readings of the Hardy Boys, how they were always slinking in fog-enshrouded doorways. Boys still slink in doorways, and alleys, and the back rooms of bars.

◆

Charlton calls. "Long time, no see," he sings out. "What have you been doing with yourself?"

"You don't want to know," I say.

"That bad, huh?" he says.

"Yes . . . well, not really. It's been okay. My date with the boy from the computer went really well—"

"Is it big?" Charlton cuts in.

"As a matter of fact, yes. But that's not what's important—"

"Not important? Silly boy, it's one of the most important things," Charlton jokes.

"You old size queen," I say. "Anyway, the date went really well, and work has been going well. I've got too many manuscripts to edit, and too many author lunches to do, but otherwise it's fine. But you know I hate talking about work. How have you been?"

"Oh, I'm a bit jumpy this week, because I have my annual checkup, making sure that I'm still cancer free. I know it's been years and years and more years, but I always get a little wacky around this type of appointment. You never know when something is going to strike. The second time I had lymphoma, they discovered it through a routine checkup. So I know that it's a possibility."

"Good God," I say. "Between you and Michael and myself, and I can't count how many others, it seems we all have some dreadful malady to worry about. And you're negative! That should give you some reassurance."

"I'm not so sure," Charlton says, "you positive boys tend to think we negs have it made, but we carry around the terrible burden of wondering if or when we're going to get infected. With you, it's a *fait accompli*, so you don't have to think about it anymore."

"I guess that's true, but we positives have to worry about dying, that's all," I say.

Charlton laughs. "And we negatives have to worry about dying, that's all. I could have a recurrence any day."

"True enough," I say. "There's no getting out of it, is there?"

"No, dear, there isn't. And we're the lucky ones on the planet. We're not living in a mud hut starving during a famine, watching our entire clan disappear to malnutrition or attacks by lions—"

"Lion attacks!" I say. "That's a good one."

"Oh, I just watched *The Ghost and the Darkness*, so I'm thinking about nature's wickedness."

"Well, you're the one to know about wickedness," I say.

"Bitch." He pauses, and I hear the click of his cigarette lighter and the soft whistle of his inhalation. "The reason I really called you, dear, is to let you know that Michael is on another downswing—"

"This week's crisis?" I say, too sarcastically.

"Yes, I know, I know . . . but the point is, Mama Jones is just not up to her usual vigor, and the place — and Michael — is suffering because of it. I think we should organize a little cleanup party, raid the apartment on Saturday and act like anal-retentive wizards. What do you say?"

"Of course," I say, "I can do that. But what's wrong with Mad Mama?"

"I don't know what's wrong with her. Michael thinks she's depressed. But I'm not so sure. I was over there last week, and Mama looked a little pale—"

"How does a black person look pale?" I ask.

"Well, maybe not pale. That's just a turn of phrase. Not her usual color? Kind of washed-out looking, piqued."

"Has she seen a doctor?" I ask.

"No, not yet. I asked her that, but she said she was going to go the women's clinic next week. She thinks it's a woman thing, because she's had some cramping, some bloating, a little bleeding . . . you know, personal bleeding, down there."

"I know what you mean," I say. "I'm not a child."

"No, you're definitely not a child, dear," Charlton says. "You haven't seen childhood in a very long time."

"You never miss a chance to take a dig, do you?" I say.

"Of course not, dear. If I did miss a chance, everyone would be all over me, filled with bitter criticism that I am not upholding the stereotype . . . no, the icon . . . no, the archetype . . . of the sharp-tongued, witty, catty old queen. It's a dying art, you know."

"Yes, I think it is," I agree. "Just the other day, I learned, to my dismay, that Scotty and Kent had never heard of felching, and they'd never heard the term 'packing fudge.' Can you imagine the naiveté?"

"Shocking, darling, just shocking," Charlton exhales a long, deep sigh. I envision a funnel cloud of blue smoke swirling around his head. "So do you want to arrange the cleaning frenzy, or should I?"

"No, I'll do it, because I was planning to go there anyway. I'll just give Mama a call."

"Okay, that's good. I've got too many calls to make. Just leave me a message about the time, what time we can be there."

And we hang up.

◈

I write in my journal:
> Something doesn't feel right about my life. This is not news. This is an ongoing problem. And has been for some time. I'm going to be forty next year, and I'm still caught up in confusing thoughts and emotions about what it is to be gay, or queer, what it means not to be young anymore. My looks are going, there's no doubt about that. But I know, too, that it's not as bad as I feel it is. So I'm a little softer than I used to be. So I'm broadening in the waist. So what? Do these things really matter?
>
> Of course not, yet they drive me in circles, around and around again, my mind protesting the onset of adulthood, protesting the superficiality of placing any importance whatsoever on something as simple and natural as gaining a little weight as I get older, or seeing my skin as less glowing than it was in my twenties. Or thirties. How can I be so shallow as to think these things matter?
>
> And yet, I am driven by these concerns. When I go to the gym and look around, I am struck by the immensity of sheer beauty there. Perfect bodies. Perfect faces. Big dicks in the showers. Friendly guys. I realize that in fact, I am part of that tableau as well, but I never really feel that I'm

a part of it all. I feel apart, separated from these others by some huge valley.

All around me I see illness and death, even with the new treatments. Sure, the deaths have slacked off, and many people I'd thought weren't going to make it have reversed their conditions and are thriving, healthy even. Michael, I think, won't make it, though, and that fact alone is enough to destroy my balance. When is it ever going to stop? When is there going to be a real cure, so that we can all get on with our lives?

But the new treatments mean that I, too, now have a (supposed) future. I never thought I'd live to see forty, and now I have to think about the possibility that I may see fifty after all. What do I want to be doing at fifty? Where do I want to be? How do I set goals when all my adult life has been spent in simply awaiting the end of my life?

But this is not what's bothering me, not really. I think I've come to accept the epidemic as a sort of everyday thing. Something to live with. Something to ignore, most of the time.

What is bothering me? If only I could pin it down, then perhaps I could wrestle with it, come up with some answers, some solutions, some goals. I guess this is why I'm in therapy. I should give it a chance, see where Dr. Kiljoy takes me in this inner journey. Inner journey? Did I write that? Am I becoming a New Age nitwit?

Michael agrees that it will be okay for Charlton and I to come over and help around the place on Saturday. We settle on noon, and I call Charlton to let him know. I ask after Mama Jones, and Michael tells me that she is still feeling unwell. It will be a big help for us to clean up and do some chores, errands.

Mad Mama Jones, whose real name is Cherise Alicia Jefferson-Jones (which explains nothing about how she came to be called Mad Mama), is a native of the Bay Area, born and raised in Berkeley. Her earliest memories are of the student anti-war riots in the late 1960s, when she was coming into awareness. She has, as a result, always seen the world as one of injustice and turmoil, a world in which one must fight and struggle to uphold one's beliefs and personhood. And like many with a fierce spirit, she has adopted a skeptical, even humorous, approach to things — she seems a lighthearted woman, though she is deeply, vibrantly aware of life's difficulties.

Being a product of the Bay Area, she also grew up with a sense of independence, of the need for self-identity, the liberating sensibility that one must define one's life as one sees fit. Formal social roles, societal expectations, stereotypes — all these mean nothing to her. She is a lesbian (sometimes) who often sleeps with men. Years ago, when she was a young woman in her twenties, she was involved (embroiled) in a number of relationships — a lesbian live-in lover, a male part-time lover, a girlfriend, and a gay boy who loved to be topped by her and her hefty strap-on.

At one point in her mid-twenties, her aunt died and left her a few thousand dollars, which she used to open a small, trendy cafe: Mad Mama's African Tea House. The cafe had been a wild success for a couple of years, but when the trend died down, she had to close the place and declare bankruptcy.

For a short while she worked at a variety of jobs, none satisfactory: bookstore clerk, telephone sales, stripper. When she volunteered to take calls at the suicide hotline — a passion born of her father's suicide when she was five — she realized that she would love to be in health care. So she set out to become a nurse and finished her RN work in a dizzyingly short time.

Her brief stints as a nurse in an old folks' home, then in a hospice, proved to her that institutional work did not suit her. Home health care appealed to her — she liked to see her patients in their domestic circumstances.

When Michael became terribly ill, two years ago — pneumonia, anemia, MAC, and cryptosporidium — it was Mad Mama Jones who was sent from the agency to care for Michael. They got on famously at once, and it was only a matter of weeks before they agreed that, in exchange for ongoing home care, Mama could share, rent-free, Michael's and Thomas's flat.

And she has been a tremendous help. It's apparent to everyone around Michael that Mama Jones is, almost single-handedly, responsible for his amazing longevity. Were it not for her careful, nurturing attentions, Michael would probably have succumbed already.

Her energy — vitality, spunk, chutzpah — has been an enduring touchstone for all of us. Which is why, of course, her current lethargy and fatigue are so worrying. Clearly, something is wrong, something more than depression or a lingering blue mood. According to Michael and Charlton, Mama has complained of sporadic bleeding and a vague abdominal discomfort. Mild indigestion — or a feeling of cramping and bloat — coupled with fatigue are the complaints that most annoy her.

I wonder what could be wrong, but Charlton's assurance that she is going to go to the women's clinic gives me some relief. It seems inconceivable that, given all our troubles, Mama Jones should suffer physical problems as well. It's just too unfair.

The Saturday cleanup fest puts us all together, though Scotty and Kent can donate only an hour, due to a previous plan to drive with friends to Muir Woods for a picnic, an hour that they devote to collecting the garbage, sorting out the recyclables, and hauling it all down to the garage for pickup.

When Charlton and I arrive, Mama is applying a cool, damp washcloth against Michael's forehead, to fight a raging fever. Mama sighs and asks Michael, "Is there anything more I can do for you?"

Michael shakes his head and says, "No, nothing. I'd really like to rest for a while."

We — Charlton, Mama, and I — withdraw and go into the kitchen, where Scotty and Kent have just bagged the last of the aluminum soda cans. I study Mama, and see, with some dismay, that Charlton is right — her color is bad. She has circles under her eyes, appears rather drawn, and she sighs a great deal. I have never seen her looking so bad.

"You're looking marvelous," I say to Mama.

"Thanks, but you must need a new prescription for your contacts. I look like hell."

Yes, you do, I think. But I don't say this. "Maybe you're a bit tired . . ."

"Oh, you queen. Don't ever call me tired. You can say that I look fatigued, or unrested, or anything else, but I am *not* tired!"

"I beg your pardon, your highness," I say.

Charlton chips in, addressing himself to Mama Jones, "Don't mind him, but do you have some vodka around here? I'd like to make myself a Long Island iced tea!"

"Alcoholic," Mama says, fetching the bottle from the cabinet. "Well, if you all are drinking, I can see what kind of a cleaning-up party this is going to be."

"Why don't you take a load off your feet," Charlton says, "and let us worry about the details. We're here to help you as much as help Michael."

She does not protest, but merely shrugs her shoulders and ambles off to her room. Charlton looks in on her after he finishes his drink, and she is fast asleep.

"Snoring!" he declares, as he returns to the kitchen. I have begun to scrub the countertops and sink. "Let's get this over with." He takes up the broom and heads for the hall. I keep at my scrubbing, polishing the windows, too, and arranging the pots and pans in an orderly way. I have a dark feeling, brooding almost, and no matter how hard I scrub, or how thoroughly I establish order among the utensils, I cannot shake the feeling.

How can I be surrounded by people who are sick, dying, and depressed? Is there no one who is healthy and energetic, no one who wakes in the morning feeling refreshed and eager to greet the day?

Since I've never felt this way, even as a child, I conclude that my fantasies of rest and renewal, energy and enthusiasm are the product of advertising. What is it that Buddhists say? "Life is suffering."

The afternoon wears on, and neither Mama Jones nor Michael make an appearance. They don't even wake up as I run the vacuum over the rugs. At long last, we finish, and Charlton rolls his eyes heavenwards and declares, "Next time let's hire a service to do this for them. I'm pooped."

"Scat queen," I say.

When I get home, Scotty and Kent are in their room quarreling. Again. I sigh and station myself just inside the kitchen door to eavesdrop.

. . . I don't care what you say, Kent shouts, *because what you do is much clearer. You wanted to get it on with Mark, didn't you? You were trying to think of a way to drag him behind some enormous redwood and ravish him, or have him ravish you . . .*

Ravish? I think. What is Kent reading these days? Gothic romances?

SCOTTY: . . . *and so what if I did want to? And so what if I did drag him behind a tree and do him. What difference does it make? It wouldn't mean anything . . .*

KENT: . . . *that's what you always say about your fucking around on the side, but if it doesn't mean anything, then why can't you just give it up? . . .*

SCOTTY: . . . *since it doesn't mean anything, then why should it matter to you? . . .*

KENT: . . . *because it makes me crazy to think of you with another guy . . . it just seems to me that if you really, truly loved me, then you'd want to give up something that makes me feel bad, especially since you say it doesn't mean anything . . .*

SCOTTY: . . . *you know what I mean . . . it doesn't mean anything to us as a couple, means nothing emotionally at all . . . you're just trying to control me—*

KENT: . . . *and why would I want to do that? . . .*

SCOTTY: . . . *because it's the only thing you know to do . . . you got these fucked up messages from your family or friends or society or I-don't-know-where, and that message makes you equate sex with love, and, more importantly, you've been programmed to think that important relationships, deeply familial relationships are all about control and sacrifice, loyalty and sexual fidelity . . .*

KENT: . . . *that's just a cop-out, and you know it . . .*

SCOTTY: . . . *why is it a cop-out for me to think originally, for me to want, to strive, to construct my life and my relationships in the best way I see how . . .*

KENT: . . . *but what about my wanting to construct a relationship that's not like what you want to construct . . .*

SCOTTY: . . . *then you shouldn't be with me, it's simple, I will not be controlled, I will not have my sex life dictated to me, this is my body, these are my urges, this is how I live my life . . .*

KENT: *. . . but you don't take into account my feelings, or my safety . . . what about safety? . . . what about you bringing home some kind of STD or something . . . not to mention, of course, the big HIV . . .*

SCOTTY: *. . . god, you're getting ridiculous, people can play safely in or out of a relationship . . . the reason this bothers you is because you want to have unsafe sex with me . . . so what kind of message is that? . . . you eagerly jumped into unsafe sex with me from the very first date, it didn't bother you then . . . you're using the safesex thing as a smokescreen . . .*

I've heard enough. It's the same argument they've been having for the entire length of their relationship, about a year and a half now. I'm tired of hearing it, living with it. They're really sweet guys, but they've both got their heads screwed on the wrong way about all this. Maybe it's better to just be positive and get on with things.

I go in my room and shut the door.

❖

I check my messages, pleased to find a cute, rambling message from Anson. Just what I need, definitely. *I just wanted to let you know that . . . no, I mean, I just wanted to invite you to spend the night at my place . . . since you've not been here yet . . . but is that maybe too fast? Should we go to a movie or something first, so it doesn't seem too . . . too . . . Oh, well, call me back when you get home . . . if you want to, that is.*

He's worried that it's too, too tawdry to do nothing but go over to his place and jump in the sack, as though we weren't really dating, just fucking. But I can think of nothing else that I'd rather do than hop into bed with Anson, so I call and eagerly accept. I still have the ability to be enthusiastic about something, after all.

7

The remnants of a tropical storm over the Pacific, down near Mexico, are blowing north, all the way to San Francisco. The sky is a brilliant, burnished blue, punctuated by massive black clouds, the atmosphere heavy with the dank air of the tropics. A rare treat, this, for San Francisco. I hear the cry of the wild parrots in the palms, the rush of warm wind down the hill, rattling my windows. I wonder what San Francisco would be like if it were a tropical port.

I rise early, unable to sleep. Vivid dreams and nightmares. Feverish and flushed. The heaviness in the air is oppressive. Today is a therapy day, which means only a half day at the office. Perhaps today's session will help lighten this gloomy mood.

I put Nine Inch Nails on the stereo, then Sleep Chamber as I dress for work. Not the kind of thing to cheer me up, but fitting for today's heavy mood. I choose all black clothes, as usual, but today they seem more appropriate than ever.

Dr. Kiljoy is wearing an elegant navy linen suit. She has opened the windows, yet the office remains stuffy. The tropical air is still, no wind whatsoever. The brooding thunderheads have stopped moving across the sky. They remain motionless, stationary. Brilliant light streams through the open windows. In the distance, I can hear the rat-tat-tat of a crew tearing up the street somewhere.

Dr. Kiljoy seats herself and gives me a hard look. I'm disconcerted by this . . . this stare. Is she angry about something?

"How did it go with Dr. Quackenbush?" she asks.

"It went okay," I answer. "We didn't really talk for very long, and then he prescribed Wellbutrin, which I've already begun taking. But I don't notice any difference."

"It will take about a month before the medication kicks in," she says, matter-of-factly. "But within a couple of weeks, you might feel some slight improvement. By four weeks you'll be well on your way."

"Well, that's fine with me," I say. "I'll try just about anything to adjust this, this . . . this bad mood. Geez, I think I was born in a bad mood."

She smiles, disarming me. I guess she's not mad about anything. I can be so paranoid. She shifts in her seat, that odd little movement that appears to be an adjustment to remedy her underclothes riding up or something. She takes up her notepad and jots something down.

"And how else was your week?" she asks.

"Not bad, I guess. Although Michael isn't doing very well. Charlton and I and . . . well, the whole group, really . . . went over to his place this last weekend and helped clean up, put things in order. His live-in friend and nurse has got something, she's sort of sick, so we all pitched in." I stop, looking down at the floor. For a moment I am filled with doubt and apprehension. What am I doing here? What was the point of starting therapy?

"What are you thinking?" she asks.

"Oh, nothing," I say. I cough and shift in my chair. "Well, truthfully, I was having a bit of doubt, or confusion, about why I'm here. I can't remember why I decided to try therapy again. The point of it is lost."

She nods and lays her notepad down. "You wanted to talk about a number of things — age, youth, looks, illness, grief, depression, your changing moods."

"Put that way," I say, "it sounds like a treasure trove of troubles, doesn't it?"

"Not especially," she says.

I wonder what she means, 'not especially'? Does she means that it doesn't sound like a lot of troubles? Or does she mean that these concerns aren't really troubles at all? Does she mean that this is common, everyday stuff that afflicts everyone?

I decide it is the last, the only choice that delivers me from self abasement and normalizes my concerns.

"Oh, yes, I remember," I say. "I think the main thing is this business of aging. Maybe it's as simple as living in a culture that worships youth, that places lesser and lesser value on people as they get older and older—"

"Yes, we do," she cuts in. "But that doesn't mean that your issues are resolved, simply by understanding that our culture is decidedly abject in this regard. Your worries are shared by many, certainly, yet you yourself must work through them, must move to a position in which you are not uncomfortable with yourself."

I think about this, pondering the sudden sense of reassurance I feel.

"You know," I begin, "last year I lost one of my dearest friends, a gay man who was ten years my senior, a man who had done everything, been everywhere. No matter what it was, he always made it safe to ask about things. He'd experienced it all, and always knew, as they say, where I was coming from."

She nods and makes a slight grimace of sympathy. God, how I hate that look, on anybody, sympathy. Is there any uglier emotion?

"When he died, I lost a valuable friend, one who I could always ask about anything, to whom I could say anything. He always knew what I was talking about, because he'd been there.

"And now he's gone, and I find myself aching for someone to talk to, someone older, more mature, who knows the score about life, about being queer, about how things are in this world."

She is still nodding her head in a gesture of deep understanding. Maybe she's for real, I tell myself.

"You're talking about a mentor," she says.

"Exactly!" I declare. "That is the precise word, thank you. Mentor. Mentoring. That's what I don't have in my life anymore. Oh, I know some people who are older than me, but they don't act as mentors, they haven't done everything, which it seemed Cap — my friend that died — had done. As a matter of fact, one of them comes to me for advice and support all the time, and he's fifteen years older than me. In a way, Charlton plays some role like that, but we're clearly more a pair of friends than we are mentor and . . . what would the word be? . . . mentee?"

She laughs. "I'm not sure what the word would be. Mentee sounds rather strange, doesn't it?"

"It does, yes," I say. "So you see, I feel I've been left in the dark, flailing my way through this aging business without anyone to steer me through it. Perhaps, though, that's part of the growing up thing, to learn to steer oneself through one's own tempests. What do you think?"

"Well, it certainly is a wonderful thing to have a mentor, and yes, learning, through life's experience and lessons, to guide oneself along one's chosen path, is one of the hallmarks of adulthood. But so is knowing when to ask for guidance, for help."

"I mean, to repeat myself, I'm going to be forty next year, and I'm not a kid anymore. No way can I be forty and think of myself as a kid, a youth. Forty means adulthood, right?"

"You are without a doubt grown up," she agrees. "And you are facing the challenges that an adult faces. One of those challenges, as you have articulated, is the wisdom of knowing oneself, knowing when to ask for assistance, knowing when to lead someone else through a problem, developing an awareness of the more subtle, but richer, dilemmas of life."

I heave a sigh of relief. "I'm so glad to hear you say that, because I am, obviously, very confused about how I should act as an adult. But not in the sense of behavior, but in the sense of understanding the meaning of things, the purpose of life, of my life especially."

"Tell me, when you were growing up," she asks, "did you feel that the men around you were mentors? That they gave you a sense of leadership?"

Her question stumps me. "What do you mean?"

"I mean," she says, "did you have role models in your father, or uncles, or the other men around you?"

"Well, I had my stepfather, but I wouldn't say he was a role model or a mentor."

"Why not?" she asks.

"Because I never liked him. I always knew that he didn't like me, didn't really like me. He married my mother, but I think he had to take us kids on as part of a package deal, so to speak. I remember once, when I was maybe six or seven, telling my mother as she tucked me in for the night, that I thought my 'dad' didn't like me. Apparently she went into the living room and repeated this to him, because in a few minutes he came into my room, sat on the edge of the bed, and said that my mom had told him that I didn't think he liked me. Then he said that he wanted me to know that, really, he loved me very much, and that he was very proud to have me as his son.

"And I remember so clearly, so, so clearly, that I knew every word he spoke was a lie. I knew he didn't love me and didn't care about me. Just how badly he didn't care wasn't apparent to me for years and years. In fact, it's only in the last few years that I have remembered, with clarity, just how miserable he was, as a man, and as a father-figure.

"He never took me to ball games, or even played catch with me in the back yard. He was a completely absent person. Oh, he was around, all right, and he would mete out my punishments, but he wasn't really there, his heart was not in it. And

I always had this strong awareness that I wasn't his real child. I was his stepson. He didn't care."

"But what about your older brother Jake?" she asks. "Was he someone you looked up to?"

"Yes, and no," I say. "I adored him, had a crush on him, that I later realized was sexual. But he was a lousy guy, very straitlaced and proper, not the wild, sort of reckless brother that the other boys had. I felt, between him and my stepdad, that I had been completely short-changed, that I had been cheated, that I was not like the other boys, whose dads and brothers took them fishing and to games, that sort of thing.

"Of course, today, looking back, I'm not sure I would have liked those things anyway, because I was truly different, because I was a little queer kid. There was no doubt about it. But I would have liked to have the chance to dislike baseball, or sports, or fishing, or whatever. I was never even given the chance to reject those things. They weren't made available to me.

"And for years, I resented that. Sometime around ten years ago, I realized that I probably wouldn't have liked those things. I liked playing with girls, with dolls, with jacks. The only boy-things I liked were Tonka trucks and GI Joe, and that's because I thought GI Joe was a hunk. He was the man I wanted to have in my life, as father, brother, whatever."

She nodded and was starting to write notes again. "Go on," she urged.

"It's interesting you asked that question . . . a minute ago, I said my dad was the one who punished me, not my mom, and I also said that it was years later that I realized how bad of a father he was . . ."

She looks up at me, because I have stopped abruptly. "Please continue," she says.

"Well, it was a byproduct of getting into the program — you know, AA and all that stuff. My denial fell away, and I was able to remember my childhood as it really was, not as the rosy, hazy childhood I had come to envision as my own. And one of the big, troubling memories was of the bizarre nature of his punishment. He would always approach me when no one was home, and he would say something like 'your mother and I feel you should be punished' for such-and-such, whatever, that they felt was a mistake and a transgression of some sort. Then he would make me strip naked, completely, and then turn me over his knee and proceed to beat the living daylights out of me. He would reach underneath me, to adjust my little boy's genitals against his thigh, and then wallop me some more.

"There was, of course, the pain of the spanking, but there was also the strange, warm pleasure of those big hands on my dick, pushing and adjusting. Whatever he was doing, at the time, I didn't know any different. But later, when I was getting clean and sober, it occurred to me like a lightning strike that he had actually perpetrated this insane little ritual.

"At the time I had these memories, I called my mother and, in a roundabout way, asked her did she remember any of these punishments, for these supposed transgressions — because I often didn't know what the hell he was talking about that I had done wrong. She became quite hysterical as I questioned her further, finally explaining the whole thing to her, and she was just beside herself with rage. She'd had no idea that any of this was going on.

"I don't suppose it sounds like much, not compared to what other kids have gone through. When you sit in AA meetings for years, and hear all these people's stories, you begin to thank the gods that your childhood was only this bad, not that bad."

"But still, it's very troubling, isn't it?" she says. She has laid her notepad on the side table again and is listening to me very closely. "Tell me, did any of this affect you at the time? What did you think, as a little boy, was going on?"

"I think, maybe . . ." I hesitate as I probe my own mind, my emotions. "I think this is why I knew he didn't really like me. Some part of me knew this wasn't normal, that he was making these stories — these transgressions — up, fabricating them. I couldn't understand it, but I think it made me distrust men, in general. They were so strong, physically, and they could inflict so much pain, and they could do it in this context of utter nonsense. It was truly like being tortured. Day and night, I never knew when he would approach me for one of these punishment sessions, and try as I might to be a good boy, I could never be good enough.

"That's when I started to light fires. I guess it's a little weird to remember that I was a child arsonist, but there it is. I was lighting fires in the yard, around the house, behind the wood pile, at church. I nearly burned the church down once, but the fire department got there too soon. I was awfully disappointed."

She has made another note. I'm sure my confession of arson is just too good to pass up.

"So to answer your original question, no, I didn't see my stepfather or my older brothers as role models. And I didn't look up to — or trust — any other men or older boys. And as far as older boys go, my dad's secretary's son used to play torture games with me."

I stop talking, ask if I can have a glass of water. She gestures to the water cooler beside the door, and I take a paper cup and pour myself one, then two, cups of cool water.

Thus fortified, I go on:

"He, the older boy, would call these games Nazi Concentration Camp—"

And here I hesitate, remembering what Charlton told me about her background, her family's annihilation in the death camps. But I go on, realizing that I must tell the truth, despite any pain I might cause her. Besides, I wasn't supposed to know anything about her personal history anyway.

"He would make me take off all my clothes, while he remained fully clothed. Then I had to display myself for him, in what I see now as fairly humiliating postures. But at the time, it was strangely exciting, and it felt good. Then he would take my little erection in his hand — because this game always gave me an erection, I derived a great deal of sexual satisfaction from it, which has always made me wonder about why everyone's always talking about protecting our children from sexuality, because all little kids grow up intensely sexual . . . but I'm rambling, off the track . . . Oh, I've lost the thread . . ."

"You were saying that this boy would take your erect penis in his hand . . ." she reminds me.

"Oh, that's right," I say. "He would grasp it and squeeze and pull as hard as he could. While he would do this, he'd ask me if it hurt yet, does it hurt? Does this hurt? He'd ask and squeeze and pull harder, until he reached my limit, and then I'd say yes, it hurts, and then he'd squeeze harder before letting me go. Eventually, I came to love this game, to crave the physical sensations it created in me, and I would seek him out. Whereas he used to force this game on me, in the beginning.

"But overall, in general, I think this only reinforced my suspicion about men and older boys, that they always had something to do with physical pain, with torture, with unfairness, with strange, unexplainable, uncomfortable — and sometimes — highly pleasureful feelings.

"I didn't trust them, any of them."

She shakes her head. "I understand. What an awful way to grow up."

I can't tell if she's genuinely expressing her concern and sympathy, or if she is posturing. I assume the former.

I get up to get more water, drink it down, and return to the chair. I see that clouds have obscured the sun, rendering the milky light in the room to a dull, monochromatic grey.

"Tell me," she says, "have you given much thought, lately, as an adult, to what it means to be a man?"

"A what?" I ask.

"A man," she repeats. "Have you given much thought, now that you're grown up, to what being a man means to you?"

I'm silent. Shifting gears. Being a man? I wonder just what she means. I tap my foot, cross my legs, uncross them, sit up straight, then slouch in the chair and cross the other leg. I make a funny face, then realize I'm stalling for time. I don't understand the question. Or rather, I *tell* myself I don't understand the question.

"I don't understand," I say.

She nods and says, "Now that you're no longer a little boy, or even a young man, have you thought much about yourself as an adult man, a grown up *man*, not a boy, not a gay man, not a queer, but just as a man?"

Her question could not be more clear, yet it discombobulates my thinking, my mind going fuzzy. I can't hold the thought, the meaning, or the substance of her question for more than a split second before it vanishes in a fog of confusion.

"What it means to be a man?" I echo.

"Yes, what it means to be a man," she repeats.

"Well . . . that's a good one . . . let me think about it for a minute."

We sit in silence. I'm supposed to be thinking about what it feels to be a man, but I can't focus on it, can't get a train of thought rolling. I keep shifting positions, clearly stalling. I take deep breaths. Dr. Kiljoy is studying my fidgeting, my nervousness.

"You know," I say, "it's not that I'm so terribly nervous, but I don't seem to be able to focus on that question."

"I understand," she says. "Why don't we move on to something else."

I feel instant relief. "Okay . . . well . . . my date with Anson went really well . . . I guess I already mentioned that last week . . ."

She nods.

"And I mentioned that Mama Jones is getting sick from something. Charlton and Scotty and Kent helped me . . . Oh, yes, Scotty and Kent are arguing again about safe sex and monogamy and all that. I'm getting very tired of having to hear their arguments. It's one of the real downsides to living with a couple. It seems, sometimes, that all couples do is either fight or fuck. Fight or fuck. That's it. Makes me wonder if I want to be in any relationship at all."

"How are you feeling about your friend Anson?" she asks.

"I feel romantic and gushy. I find it hard to believe myself, but I'm a sucker for romance. I develop crushes on a moment's notice, and I'm already having that falling-in-love feeling. I just don't want to scare him off."

"Do you think he shares your sentiments? Is he responding enthusiastically?"

"Yeah, I think so," I answer. "But we haven't had that many dates, really, only two in fact. But we talk on the phone and send sweet little e-mails to each other. God, I love this part. And it's been a long time since I was in this kind of thing. It's great and it's scary at the same time."

"Of course," she says. And that's all.

I see that it is nearly time for us to stop. "We're planning to have a cocktail party soon, me, my housemates, Charlton and everyone. It should be fun. You're welcome, but I don't suppose your professional ethics allow it, do they?"

She shakes her head. "Not really, but it would be good to see Charlton again. Do give him my greetings, won't you?"

"Yes, I will."

8

Summer is nearly over, and we are approaching fall, my favorite time of year. Everything has shifted, from cool, summer fog to warm, hazy days and earlier nightfall, a snap in the air, decidedly autumnal. Soon, rain will be on the way, intermingled with days of intense, hot sunshine, and nights as crisp and brittle as peppermint candy.

That rusty, sodden, moldy odor of fall is in the air, especially after dark. The smell of decay, of leaves piling up, dampness rotting everything. The same smell I remember from the tropics, in Mexican jungles, Hawaiian grottoes, New Orleans, Martinique, Trinidad. I breathe deep of that scent. Sweltering, humid.

❖

We all talk on the phone endlessly, volunteering (or being volunteered) for various tasks in association with the upcoming cocktail party. We phone our invitations, as we've decided to hold the party this very weekend, no time to mail invitations.

As the day for the party approaches, I am tense, on edge (as always). Deadlines — even good, eagerly anticipated deadlines — provoke in me an urgency, an air of expectation that feels like anxiety. The work week slips away, offering relief as I bury myself in a manuscript about ancient Egyptian magic, fascinating stuff, but the writing is horrendous. I have to have a handful of red pencils to edit the damn thing. I invite Mariah, one of the assistant editors to the party, and tell her, too, to bring along her girlfriend Dale. We'll need some lesbians at the party, though I don't think that Mariah and Dale consider themselves to be lesbians. I think they, like myself, prefer to be categorized, if we must, as queer.

I wake trembling the morning of the party, unsure (as I often am) where I am, what room this is, what city. As I rub the sleep from my eyes, it all comes clear to me, and I am focused on the one (and only) task I must do: get ice.

It's nearly eight o'clock, and Michael, and his lover Thomas, are arriving with Mad Mama Jones. Getting Michael upstairs and situated on the couch, a glass of sparkling water within easy reach, is a gargantuan chore that leaves us panting. We literally have to carry Michael upstairs. "However did you get him down at your place?" I whisper to Mama Jones, incredulous. "You don't want to know," she says, winking. "I had to ring the neighbors' flat and beg them to help Thomas and I to get Michael into the car. We really just carried him down, packed him in the car like a sack of potatoes. I tell you, this business has got to end soon. I'm not up for it any longer."

I nod knowingly and then shake my head. "What a tough time you're having. Please, please call us whenever you need anything at all." Mama nods and whispers Thank You.

Scotty and Kent appear from the kitchen, where they have been putting ready-made hors d'oeuvres in the oven, opening packages of cookies, and laying out the bar. They rush to Michael and perch themselves around him, a little too solicitously, it appears to me, but Michael doesn't seem to notice, reveling in the attention and the sheer change of scene. Thomas slinks into the kitchen, then goes in search of the bathroom.

Mama and I go into the kitchen and pour ourselves glasses of wine. Mama raises her eyebrows at me. "I thought you were sober?"

"I am," I say. "Completely on the wagon except for a glass of wine now and then, maybe a beer on a hot day, and of course champagne on New Year's. Otherwise, I'm completely sober."

"Well keep it up!" Mama says, sarcastically or proudly (I can't tell which).

The doorbell rings and I rush to buzz them in — them turning out to be Charlton and his new blond boyfriend, whose name I can't recall. "Darling, you look stunning,"

Charlton says, giving me exaggerated French-style kisses in the air to either side of my face. "I'm glad you made it, and early, too!" I say, turning to smile at what's-his-name, extending my hand to him.

"This is Derek," Charlton introduces, "the infamous blond. This will be something of a debut for him."

Derek (a strange name for a blond, I think, but of course do not say) shrugs, smiles, and shakes my hand. "How do you do?" he says. How formal of him, I think. He must be from the East Coast. But then, who's ever heard of a natural blond coming from back East?

I wave them along the hall and lead them to the kitchen. "Fix anything you want to drink, and eat anything you like."

"Including the guests?" Charlton says, laughing.

"Trash," I say, heading in the direction of the bathroom, which I see is unoccupied. Thomas has apparently gone down the hall, to one of the bedrooms, or perhaps the library. I decide to leave him be. It is undoubtedly a real treat for him to find some time, even a few minutes, to himself. The pressure of Michael's unremitting and unresolvable illness must be — is — smothering.

So I make my way back to the living room, where Scotty and Kent are deep in conversation with Michael, and Mama Jones is taking a pick (fairly frantically) to the block of ice. Charlton and what's-his-name are settling themselves into the large sofa and grabbing (fairly greedily) at the pretzels. The doorbell rings, and I buzz in Mariah and Dale.

Greetings are exchanged, and Mama urges them to mix vodka gimlets, introducing herself as Michael's nurse, which fails to register with Dale, but Mariah explains to her the connections of our little group. Mariah gravitates to Charlton, engaging him in a conversation about the weakness in the new color press in Japan. What's-his-name smiles and begins to chat with Dale, and I see that they are hitting it off.

So far, so good.

The last to arrive is Anson, and I'm relieved that he has, indeed, arrived. In the entry hall, we grab each other and suffocate ourselves in a series of passionate and almost too needy kisses. I swoon and consider taking him into the bedroom straightaway. But no, that will not do.

Instead I lead Anson to the living room, the heart of our little party. Introductions are made all around, no one remembering anyone's names. The usual lighthearted jokes are made about a name quiz. But for a small gathering, it seems very congenial, surprisingly so. Everyone has broken up into little conversation groups, and the booze is flowing freely.

As the evening progresses, it seems a certain frivolity sets in, at this friendly fest. But it is apparent, too, that no one wants to admit (or acknowledge, or betray) the facts that both Michael and Mama Jones look utterly haggard. Yet the party remains convivial, even gay, laughter ringing out, people wandering off alone to explore the flat.

At one point, as I pour myself another glass of (sober) wine, I hear Charlton saying something about some Hollywood personality being ". . .gay, queer, whatever."

I step in. "Oh, Charlton, 'queer' is not a substitute for 'gay.' Queer is like all about weird hair and being quirky and non-labeled, and gay is about neon thong bikinis and going to the gym—"

"Give it a rest, Miss Thing," Mama interrupts. "I know you love getting down on your knees and honking on a nine-inch choker and I've seen you, with my own two eyes, going after any boy who has a big bulge in his pants, with your bosoms heaving and your boy-twat twitching. I'm sorry, but you can't get any more gay than that!"

This brings the party to a standstill (momentarily), and then everyone bursts into applause and laughter. "Touché, darling," Charlton says to Mama. "You certainly read his beads!"

"I believe that is my role in this life," she says.

The party resumes its original chattering gaiety, and I corner Anson, give him a kiss on the mouth. "I want to take you in the bedroom and ravish you," I say, nuzzling his neck. He holds me close and whispers, "Later, stud, later." I am aching for him.

◆

Already anticipating the end of the party and my chance to be alone with Anson, I move from person to person, group to group, appearing in the midst of conversations I do not understand. I step onto the porch to smoke a cigarette and find Mariah and Dale sharing a joint.

"Want some hooch?" Mariah, asks. I shake my head. "No, heroin would be more like it."

"What? You're not enjoying your party?" Dale says.

"No . . . I mean yes, I'm enjoying the party, I'm just horny, and Anson is here, and . . . well, you know . . ."

"Um-huh," Mariah grunts. And proceeds to deliver herself of a long, rambling (tedious) monologue about Katherine, a very large, very unpleasant woman with whom we both work. I listen with only one ear, my mind elsewhere.

Where I am going, in my mind, is back into the past, recalling with a vivid sense of *deja vu*, a party such as this — just like this — when I was with Edward, a party that felt precisely the same but was populated by a completely different set of guests. It occurs to me, with some wrenching sadness, that this is the third, or perhaps fourth, generation of friends. Most, if not all, have been consumed by the epidemic. It is a moment of grief, painful in the extreme, and as fast as I touch that horrible emotion, I banish it. Not now, not here.

◆

I suddenly realize that Thomas has completely disappeared and go in search of him. I find him in the library, sitting in the great overstuffed velvet chair, reading a leather-bound copy of Gore Vidal's *Julian*. I see that he has a glass of brandy beside him. There is the delicious smell of liquor and old books.

"Is anything the matter?" I ask.

He shakes his head. "No, nothing at all. I'm actually quite happy to be here, thank you for inviting us. But I've sequestered myself because I just can't face a roomful of charming, happy people . . ." His voice trails off.

"What is it?" I whisper, truly concerned. For Thomas, in his own way, has been a solid pillar of strength throughout Michael's illness and continued failing health. Where Mama Jones has provided boundless practical support — and emotional support, too — Thomas has come to signify, or represent, the old masculine quality of silent strength. There is, even with all the grief and suffering he must endure, a profound serenity about him. I think, of course, of others I have known who have shared this quality, but it is rare, rare indeed, particularly among gay men, especially in California, where we are all encouraged to reclaim the feminine side of ourselves, to disclose every emotion, to elaborate and wax on our troubles in the belief that such blather assists us in "coping." But Thomas does not participate in this collective sentiment. Instead, he embodies an unexcited, unexcitable tranquillity. It is something I admire enormously.

I smile, put my hand on his shoulder. "I'll leave you to your reading." And then, as I turn to go, I stop and say, "You know, Thomas, that I admire the way you remain a solid rock through all these troubles."

He looks at me, our eyes locking for a moment. I see appreciation in his eyes, as well as that assuredness that he, too, recognizes his own strengths. He mouths the words Thank You, and I return to my guests.

An hour later, Michael announces that he must go home, he's too tired. Mama Jones comes to his aid, helping him to rise from the sofa, put on his jacket, and get prepared to descend the stairs and begin the difficult task of simply getting home. Scotty and Kent come to the rescue, wrapping their arms around Michael from both sides and, as Thomas and Mama follow, quite literally carry him down the stairs and into the car.

Their departure alters the mood of the party. A certain madness sets in, as though we have all been freed of some sort of constraint. Dale and Mariah begin to play charades with Scotty and Kent. Anson begins to cling to me as I chat with Charlton and what's-his-name.

Charlton, being his usual self, leers at Scotty and Kent, saying, "What I wouldn't give to be in a sandwich with them! Especially Scotty. What an ass. He's sitting on a gold mine."

"Well, he used to hustle," I say. "And he was very good at it."

"I knew that," Charlton says, "I just wish I'd hired him when he was still working. That butt! So munchable! And it seems to have a life of its own. Oh, am I being vulgar?"

What's-his-name, Derek, is annoyed by this exchange. And I don't blame him. It seems a bit rude for Charlton to be leering at Scotty while holding the hand of this beautiful blond boy. I see, too, that Scotty has somehow overheard these remarks and is frowning, momentarily failing to participate in the game of charades. Uh-oh, I think, trouble.

And, with a flash of intuition, I know that Charlton and Derek will have words about this later. The angry glint in Derek's eye speaks volumes about his attitudes and beliefs about relationships. Clearly, he does not cotton to Charlton's freewheeling, obvious lustiness. But then, it is also apparent that Charlton has had too much to drink, and perhaps, I think (hopefully), Derek will understand this and forgive Charlton his lewd remarks.

I surprise myself with this line of thought. It's unlike me to consider anything as lewd or inappropriate, but something about the sad anger in Derek's expression — shown for just an instant — touches my heart, and I feel sorry for him. I do not know this boy, but I can see, can intuit, that he cares (already) deeply for Charlton. This, I think, is worth consideration, respect, and a little restraint.

The party madness dissipates as we approach midnight. I see Mariah yawning out on the deck, cigarette (or joint) in hand. Dale approaches her and they whisper. A moment later, they appear, their jackets in hand, bidding everyone goodnight and thanking Scotty, Kent, and I for the evening.

When they leave, Charlton and Derek take their lead, and gathering their coats, they, too, take leave of the party. So now, it is only Scotty and Kent and Anson and I. We all pitch in to clean up — picking up glasses, napkins, paper plates. Emptying the bowls of pretzels and chips. Throwing the uneaten hors d'oeuvres in the garbage.

This tidiness accomplished, Scotty and Kent go out to go dancing at a club, leaving Anson and me alone in the flat.

He turns to me and smiles, a devilish grin. We fall upon each other immediately, like hungry animals, tearing at our clothes, kissing and grasping, groping and pulling, doing just about anything that two men can do together. As if we've just discovered our bodies, and sex, for the first time.

Later, as we lay in bed, I hear Anson's slow breathing. Asleep already. As usual, I remain awake for a long time, reviewing the evening, thinking (happily) about Anson, about how lucky I am to have him, to have my friends. Does life get any better than this?

The next day, Anson and I pack a picnic lunch and head out to the beach at Land's End. We laugh when we see the warning sign, so poetically rendered: "Dangerous surf area. People have been swept from the rocks and drowned." It is the rhythm of the sentence, and the use of the word 'swept,' that lends this poetic ring to the warning. It reminds us of *Vertigo*, and *Tales of the City*, when Michael Tolliver remarks on this very sign.

It is warm at the beach, in the sun, but the air is cool, a mild moist breeze caressing our naked bodies. The song of the surf bathes us and induces a sweet lethargy. We turn this way and that, exposing every nook and cranny to the bronzing light. To be naked outdoors, to feel the warmth of the sun on parts usually hidden, to feel the kiss of the breeze, the faint spray of the surf, on the skin — it's delicious, luxurious. A dreamy somnolence overtakes us, and we snooze, letting ourselves (unknowingly) burn.

We eat our picnic lunch — tuna sandwiches, wedges of sharp Cheddar, sweet pickles, and potato chips, washed down by sparkling Calistoga water — and then pack up our things to go. We hike back up to the parking lot, winding our way through dense shrubs, cypresses twisted and bent by the westerly sea breezes, a carpet of wild grasses underfoot. We stop many times to admire the views along the trail, the view of the Marin Headlands, of the lighthouse, of the great outcropping of towering rocks close to shore. A lone foghorn stands sentinel in the sea, at the mouth of the Golden Gate, its silence testimony to this clear, waxy sky, this liquid atmosphere of burnished azure.

"Truly," Anson says, "this is an enchanted place."

I need not say anything to agree.

Later, after a few errands — a short trip to the grocers, half an hour on the exercycle at the gym, laundering our sandy beach towels — we decide to dine on South Park, in a tiny, elegant restaurant with windows overlooking the square. It is a romantic dinner, candles and soft sourdough bread, a kind (and very handsome) waiter. We talk of very little, happy and comfortable in the presence of each other; conversation isn't necessary.

When we are done, after indulging in creme brulee and butterscotch pie, we go our separate ways, Anson to his house, me to my flat.

It has been a perfect day, a perfect weekend, actually. I putter around my bedroom, flicking the TV on and then off, listening to Chet Baker on the CD. Eventually, finally, I settle into bed, prop up the pillows and read some more of Proust, my autumn project, to read through *Remembrance of Things Past*.

My eyes growing tired, later, I set the book aside and slide between the cool sheets. I take a deep breath and luxuriate in the emotion of contentment. Such a perfect weekend seems so very much at odds with the realities of the working world, to which I must return tomorrow, to the stark work with Dr. Kiljoy, to the usual gloom of life as lived in the City, with its epidemics, its homeless beggars, its potholed streets. I banish these thoughts and let myself fall asleep.

9

Therapy again. I trudge into the Duboce Triangle, stepping around a dozen different beggars, some homeless, some just lazy bums. One man, a boy really, dressed in retro-punk gear, asks for a dollar. He's so cute that I give him one, and then feel guilty that I have responded to his cuteness, his youthful beauty. Does that make him more worthy than the other beggars? Can I be so superficial as to step over the decrepit hag who slurs the phrase spare change, sir? so that it comes out as spurzhansser? Or the obvious tweaker, jittering in front of the bus stop?

In Dr. Kiljoy's waiting room, I sit. For quite a while. She is late. Five minutes, ten, then fifteen. I am about to leave when she rushes into the room, unlocks her door, and mumbles hurried apologies about emergencies and traffic. I do not take the bait. Every therapist I've ever had has pulled this stunt, more than once. It seems they want to evoke the patient's impatience, stir up some minor irritation, just to see how the patient will react.

I do not react. I say, "Of course, it's no problem." But the usually calm, collected doctor is harried and unfocused. She smoothes her hair, brushes the back of her skirt, and takes her seat. I sit quietly and observe this rattled behavior, amused.

Suddenly, her expression shifts, she looks directly at me, her concerned therapist visage fully engaged, and says, "Again, let me apologize for being late. It's very rare for me."

"Oh, it's no problem, not at all," I say. "As a matter of fact, it gave me a few extra minutes to compose myself and think about our session."

She nods. Do I detect a tiny bit of disappointment? Was she expecting annoyance, anger?

"It's been a full week," I start. "Our cocktail party was a success, I think. Everyone seemed to have a good time. Afterwards, Anson spent the night and the next day. We had a great time, really magical, going to the beach, going out to eat, lots of good sex. I'm definitely in love with him, already, but I haven't told him."

"Do you think he feels the same way?" she asks.

"Oh, yes, I'm certain. I can't imagine that he isn't just as eager and excited about this as I am."

"That sounds very promising," she says.

Very promising? What a dry, dry phrase.

"Well, yes, I think . . ." I say, at a loss suddenly. Then, "So I do have my hopes that this is going to turn out well, that this relationship is going to have some staying power. It's very different for me to feel this way about someone. After having buried three lovers, I think I've retreated into some kind of shell, a hardened heart that's a defense against any more possible losses.

"But with Anson, it's different. I don't fear losing him. He's not sick, just positive, so that's not a current concern. But I have no fear. And that's a relief. I think I'm ready to move into a new relationship, even though I can't predict how things are going to turn out. I guess my point is, I'm now — suddenly — willing to try."

"That must feel good, refreshing?" she says, a question.

"Yes, it does," I say. "It's like a shot in the arm, better than vitamin B." I laugh. She smiles. I go on: "There's an uneasy feeling, though, I'll admit, that I've constructed an idea of what a boyfriend should be. And Anson seems to fit the 'job description' very well. It makes me wonder if I'm genuinely interested in him as a person, as someone to share life with, or if I'm just letting him fill a position I have open, like a job."

"Perhaps a bit of both?" she says. And I think, of course, yes.

"You know, I've been worrying about people this week," I start. Then stop, frowning, for reasons that are unclear to me.

"Go on," she prompts.

"Well, I think I mentioned that Mama Jones is sick with something, though we don't know what it is—"

She nods.

"And at the party, even though she was lighthearted and funny, as always, she lacked the sparkle that she usually has. I don't know why, but I have a dark feeling about this. Maybe it's because the epidemic has raged on for so long that I'm in the habit of assuming the worst."

"If you assume the worst," she says, "you can never be taken by surprise."

What kind of a response is that? I wonder. Is she presenting this aphorism as one of life's little wisdoms? She detects my hesitation, my annoyance, and says, "But yes, I agree that the epidemic has made us all jump to the worst conclusions in health matters."

Better, I think.

"I know she's going to go to the doctor next week, so I should stop worrying and just wait and see. But, like I said, I can't shake this bad feeling, like a premonition."

"And how is your friend Michael?" she asks.

"The same," I answer. "Maybe a little worse. Well . . . maybe a lot worse. Getting him to that party nearly required an act of Congress. We had to carry him up and down the stairs. But you know, the next evening, after I came home from my day with Anson, Scotty and Kent told me that during the party, they had convinced Michael to embark on a program of acupuncture and Chinese herbs. I hope he does, because it surely can't hurt, and if it helps only a little bit, that would be something.

"But I worry, of course, that he won't do anything, that he's too far gone to make much of a difference anyway. And so I worry, and worry some more."

"But what about the new therapies?" she asks.

"Oh, sure, he's tried those," I say. "But he reacted violently to them. He tried several different medications, and both times his liver and pancreas got really bad. He had to be discontinued."

"What about the old therapies?" she asks.

"Well, he's used them all up," I answer. "AZT, ddC, blah blah blah . . . he's tried them all, for years now. It doesn't seem he has any real options left."

"That's a tough one," she says. And I think she is genuinely sympathetic. At least her comment sounds heartfelt.

"What else do you worry about?" she asks.

I scrunch up my face, then say: "I'm worried about Scotty and Kent. It seems like all they do is fight and make up, fight and make up, over and over again. It's always about the same thing — monogamy. But I'm beginning to see that the monogamy issue is, maybe, a smokescreen for something bigger, something more worrisome—"

"Which is?" she prompts.

"Which is that neither of them is willing to yield. They argue till they're blue in the face, but they never resolve anything because they're not approaching it from a position of compromise. They don't negotiate. It seems, for each of them, that it must be all or nothing."

"And that troubles you?" she asks.

"Of course it does," I say, "because it means that they're not really talking, not really working towards a solution, not really loving — and supporting — each other. They're locking horns. To my point of view, that spells trouble."

"It can," she agrees. "I can certainly see that."

"I know I haven't said much about Scotty, but he's one of my shining stars, one of the people in my whole life that can make the world light up — the way I'm starting to feel about Anson. But lately, in the last six months or so, I've noticed a change in him, something reckless, obstinate. He wasn't like this before he got together with Kent. He was always flexible, tolerant, easily adaptable. This hard stance, this unyieldingness, is new, and it provokes in him a sort of belligerence that I find disagreeable."

"And how does that affect you?" she asks.

"It affects me," I say, "because he's not the same person he once was. He's harder somehow, a little meaner. And I don't understand it. How can being in a relationship make someone more edgy? I'd think it would make a person more loving, softer . . . oh, I don't know what I'm talking about . . ."

"Any other worries?"

"Yes," I say, "Charlton is going in for his annual cancer checkup next week, and I'm worried that they'll find something."

Her eyes widen at this. Of course she worries about Charlton, too.

"But I should just wait and see. He's probably just fine . . ."

I stop talking. She says nothing.

"But that's it," I start again. "That's what's really bothering me . . . not the worrying as much as the circumstances that are making me worry. Why, pray tell, am I . . . are we . . . surrounded by so much illness? Even with the new treatments, the epidemic rages on. It's great that so many people I know are getting a second chance, are doing really well, healthier and stronger than in years. And yet, it seems that every major event in my life, still, revolves around illness in one way or another, whether it's Mama Jones, or Charlton, or depression, or sobriety . . ."

"I'm afraid that life is like that sometimes," she says. "I admit that it's been a constant siege for decades now, as far as the epidemic goes. But life is about illness and death. They are the two great issues we all face, always."

"But why can't I have some major life events that aren't about illness? Why can't I win the lottery or something?"

"Well, there's Anson," she says.

I hesitate, surprised that I didn't think of that myself. "You're right, I guess. That's a major life event, isn't it? . . . or at least the possibility of one .. and that's positive, good, happy even . . ."

Neither of us says anything for a few moments. I look around the office. It seems darker than usual. Ah, the lamp in the corner is turned off, and the velvet drapes are only half open. A cozy, soothing environment.

"Last week, I asked you how you feel about being a man. You seemed to resist the question, or were confused by it. But I'd like to pursue the subject, if you will," she says.

"Okay . . . uh . . . I have given it some thought during the week," I start. "But I haven't made much progress. Frankly, it's not something I've thought much about in my life, so far, at least not in that way, in the sense of being a man. I've been thinking, in general, about what it means to be an adult, grown up, how I should conduct myself, how I should rise above my feelings, rather than be a slave to them. I'm beginning to believe that feelings . . . emotions . . . are overrated. It's just too easy to be ruled by them. It seems to me that a mark of adulthood is being able to carry on despite one's feelings, to simply note emotions when they arise and then let them go. All this dwelling on them, mulling them over, examining them this way and that . . . well, it seems too burdensome. Unnecessary, actually."

She nods her head and begins taking notes.

"I know that this grownup thing has been on my mind for a while now. It's one of the main reasons I wanted to come to therapy, you know, because, turning forty, I see that it's just not attractive to act like I'm a kid anymore. But there are all these pressures, all this pushing and pulling, I feel all around me. I go to the gym, I see all these young, exquisite beauties, with their young, perfect bodies and flawless skin and muscles bulging, and I feel inferior, because I'm not young like they are anymore.

"And then I feel silly. Why disparage the natural process of aging? Why feel that my life is over? Why worry and compare myself to guys that are at the place I was when I was their age? Why not accept things as they are, move graciously into the next phase of my life?

"And it's exactly this line of thinking that I find so unbecoming in someone about to turn forty. Surely by now I should be through with all this . . . all this superficial stuff. Surely by now I've learned something about the value of people for who they are on the inside. Right?"

I pause. She is looking at me intently. She says, "But our culture tells us that aging, that being old, is a bad thing. We all, young or old, male or female, professional or blue collar, struggle with this issue. It's ingrained in our culture. And it's peculiar to Western culture, America especially."

I nod my head, agreeing with her. At least she knows what I'm talking about, I think. But of course she does! Women feel this even more strongly than men. The pressures on a woman to remain young, pretty, and thin are enormous.

She keeps talking: "But I suspect, from what you're saying, that you already have a notion of what it means to be an adult, of the pitfalls in our culture with regard to youth and aging. What I want you to look at is your sense of yourself as a man, not a boy, not a gay boy, not an adult, but a grown man."

"I think I understand what you're trying to get at," I say. "But, as I thought about it this week, I realized I'm not sure what it is to be a man. I feel I don't even know any men, just gay boys. The men at work are all straight and really fucked up, as straight men tend to be. I can't look up to any of them. I feel I'm the most mature of the bunch."

"I'm sure you are," she says. "Gay men tend to be more mature in many ways than their heterosexual counterparts, and I believe this is because gay men — and women, too — have had to face the difficult challenge of coming to terms with their sexuality. They've had to break away from social programming, at least insofar as sexual identity goes, and that sort of development is a truly adult thing to do."

I enjoy this analysis. It makes me feel proud somehow. At least she can see the value in the experience of coming out. Of course, I had wondered if a straight woman therapist was really a good choice for me. Would she understand me? Or would she adopt a stance, a heterosexual stance, of toleration rather than empathy? She is clearly a formidable woman.

"But that's behind me now," I go on. "I need to . . ." And here my voice trails off. "I've lost the thread," I say.

"We're talking about manhood, what it means to be a man," she reminds me. "You were saying that you feel you have no role models for manhood, no one to whom you can look for inspiration, if you will."

"Well, this business about manhood is very strange," I say.

"How so?" she asks.

"Because it's not something I've ever really analyzed. And it's not something I've ever discussed with any of my friends. It's certainly not something that's discussed at a community level. The gay press, the gay mags, they don't discuss masculinity. I've always assumed, I guess, that manhood — manliness, masculinity — was something that queer men aspired to disparage, to get away from.

"I mean, being queer, or gay, or whatever, I feel allied, very strongly allied, with feminism. I can hardly consider myself a feminist if I start to take on the macho trappings of manhood. It seems just too retro."

"Then we need to take a look at the reasons why you feel that manhood and feminism pose a conflict for you."

Jesus Christ! I think. Isn't it obvious? Queer men spend a great chunk of their time and energy in life trying to shed the postures and imbecilities of manliness. False bravado, crudeness, that fake camaraderie of sports, the jokes about 'tits' and 'pussies' and all of that. Being a gay man means rejecting all of that, not embracing it.

I decide to change the subject.

We are both silent for a long moment. I can hear the ticking of the clock behind her desk. I see that we don't have much time left. Thank god for that, I think. This has been enough for one day.

"You know," I say, "I still have my doubts about this, about therapy. It's nice to clear my head a little bit, to see my problem areas, but where is the possibility of change in all this? I mean, how can talking about all these things effect any change? How can I see real transformation in my life, if all I do is talk about it?"

She nods. "Yes, I understand what you're saying, but I'm of the opinion that talking about things helps clarify them. Once your problems are clear to you, then transformation sets in. It is the first step, a sort of taking inventory of your life, your beliefs, your values, your attitudes — everything, in short, that places you firmly in the grip of who you are right now. Once you see that clearly, you can make decisions about what you want."

"I guess one of the things I did learn in the program, AA, you know," I say, "is that it takes more than thinking and talking to change your life. It takes action, it takes doing things in the here and now that will create the person you want to be tomorrow. I just don't see that therapy offers that kind of action."

"Well, there are many approaches to psychotherapy," she says, "and certainly the twelve-step approach is one that seems to work for many people. I do see the twelve-steps as a form of therapy, one that is supported by the larger group, but it is essentially, as you say, a program of taking action—"

"But where does therapy fit into all of this?" I interrupt.

"As I said, I believe that therapy is essentially a task of taking inventory, of ferreting out the things that are important to you and the things that are not important to you. If you do not lay this groundwork, transformation is simply not possible, at least in my view."

Her approach seems, on the surface, to be wise. But I'm left with a nagging sense that it's not enough, that the groundwork of therapy is simply not enough for transformation. It seems there ought to be something easier — or different — that I can do.

I do not say any of this.

What I say is: "But what do I want to transform?"

"That's a good question," she says, "and it's the question that we are trying to formulate here, in therapy, through talk, and memory, and, most importantly, understanding. But yes, I agree that one needs to be clear about what it is that one wants to transform. Can you say more about your thoughts in this regard?"

I cringe, sometimes, at the formality of her speech, each word weighed and measured. This annoys me.

"I want to be somebody else," I say, simply. "I want to wake up in the morning and feel good about myself, about my life, about my body and work and friends. I don't want to wake up and think about illness and sadness and loss and have to force myself out of bed—"

"I know," she cuts in, "and you are, again, talking about depression, about the symptoms of depression. The medication should help with that, very soon, I hope."

"But is medication the answer?" I ask. "Can it be that the anti-depressant will only mask my pain, reduce me to a numbed-out zombie who feels content, even though he is not?"

"I do not believe that is a possibility," she says. "I believe that depression is a physical problem, a matter of brain chemistry. Of course, we know that it's tied to life's events, because the events of our lives influence our brain chemistry, even the structure of our neurotransmitters. It is really as simple as that."

I ponder this statement for a few moments. My intuition tells me that this isn't true, or only partially true. My problem seems to be multi-dimensional, even if I can't put my finger on it.

◆

When I get home, I hear that the neighbors have, once again, thrown open their windows and are blasting a recording of the Gay Men's Chorus out onto the street. This is a regular, annoying practice of theirs, and I am tired of hearing the same songs over and over again. I can't imagine why they do it? Do they think that everyone in the neighborhood wants to hear this corny stuff?

10

A shimmering, brilliant autumn day, the kind that delights the soul, all warmth, the sun glaring but not burning. Soon, we will have our first storms, those gentle autumn rains that polish the atmosphere and render ensuing days as crisp, shiny, and clear as pure, clean crystal. I think, perhaps, San Francisco looks best in the fall.

Scotty has come to me, this morning, to tell me that he's worried, mightily so. He's had an episode of unprotected anal intercourse ("riding bareback" is the popular phrase these days), with a nineteen-year-old boy. As Scotty explains, the boy's dick was tremendously huge, and a condom was simply not a possibility. And the boy said he was negative, and since someone who is nineteen has probably not been infected (as Scotty said to me this morning), he thought it was okay.

But after the fact, this morning, he's nervous and preoccupied with this (potentially) risky episode. And he tells me, not surprisingly, that this isn't the first bareback experience he's had in the last year.

He doesn't know whether or not to tell Kent, because perhaps, he thinks, it's best for him to get tested quietly, and if all goes well, then Kent need not know. "But you can't keep up with these deceptions," I tell Scotty, "because it's an unhealthy dynamic in your relationship. The very thing Kent is so worried about is the very thing you've done."

Scotty concedes this point, but doesn't know what to do. He's driven, by a high sex drive, and a deep need for adventure, to seek a wide variety, and large quantity, of sexual experiences. I don't know how to advise him.

Now, as I dress for work, I notice a lightening of my mood, a strange, unfamiliar calm. This must be the anti-depressant kicking in, I say to myself. I put the Virgin Prunes on the CD, then Chris & Cosey. I gather the manuscript I've been editing, put it in my portfolio, and, ready to go, I sit still for a few minutes, looking out the window.

It's going to be warm today, I think. And then I reflect on Scotty's talk — his confession really — and wonder just what is the best course for him. If it were me, I'd tell Kent and get tested and see what happens. Because I wouldn't be able to hide so much from someone I love. But of course, honesty isn't the same as disclosure, and what Kent doesn't know won't hurt him. In some ways, I'm as conflicted about the monogamy issue as Kent and Scotty are. Well, as Kent is. His point — that Scotty's fucking around exposes Scotty to risk and then possibly exposes Kent to risk — is understandable.

And of course it's not just about HIV. It's about herpes, and the clap, and syphilis, and warts, and hepatitis, and chlamydia, and cytomegalovirus, and on and on.

But the other half of Kent's argument — that he goes crazy at the thought of his lover with another man — is insufferable, and it's there that I agree with Scotty and disagree strongly with Kent. For this argument isn't about risk, not about safety, but is about control, about a power struggle in the relationship, about codependence. Jealousy is one of the most destructive emotions, and it has nothing to do with Scotty's behavior. It has to do with Kent's fear, his fear of loss, his fear of the possibility of change, his fear of personal freedom. Such a person can't distinguish between emotional fidelity and physical activity. Sex is equated with love. And, of course, the two need have nothing to do with each other.

But then I see the clock says half past eight, so I take up my portfolio, walk out the door and down the hill to the MUNI metro. It *is* going to be very warm today, hot as a stovetop.

All this talk of sex and infection has sparked my imagination, and I decide to go out to the sex clubs. I choose a dark, sleazy club on Tenth Street, in a rickety old Edwardian building that creaks and groans, just as its patrons groan and moan. It's dark in here, and I feel mischievous (horny, wicked).

Sex at a gay men's sex club is something of an athletic event. There are so many men and boys, so many possible combinations, so many types of equipment available to accommodate a variety of taste, from glory holes to slings, bunk beds to shadowy corners, platforms and mirrors, video rooms and easy chairs.

At the door I check my shirt and jacket and begin to wander through those halls, those rooms, those mazes. Whispers and shadows pass me. Every sort of current and past gay or queer fashion is represented, from the burly mustachioed clone of yesteryear in his tight-fitting jeans to shaved-head punkboys in their loose, floppy shorts and little black boots. I love them all, punks, studs, bears, musclemen, and effete, lithe little wisps of young men.

But it is a shaved-head punkboy who catches my eye, and, as it develops, my mouth and my butt. He possesses a truly beautiful cock, I think, as I examine it up close, me on my knees. Satiny smooth, thickly veined, long — all the adjectives that are the staple of pornography. And his passion is reckless, rough. I like that, tonight, here.

Finished with him, I sit in the video room sipping a cup of coffee. I go to take a leak and discover an elderly man, creature really, kneeling beside the toilet, his thirst palpable. I do not indulge him. Instead, I walk upstairs to use that bathroom, which, not surprisingly, is utterly filthy. What is it with these places, that they can't keep the john clean, a fresh supply of paper towels, a jar of soap? Is this the third world?

Wandering the club, I find a short, compact muscle boy, thick and solid. Oh, yes, I think, and reach over to his bare chest to tease his nipple. He stiffens, and I think, oh, no, he's not interested. But then he mirrors my gesture, taking my nipples between his thumbs and forefingers and twisting exquisite pleasure into my body, driving my passion forward. He kneels and takes me in his mouth, and I feel that yes, here is a true, natural-born cocksucker — his mouth velvety soft, wondrously warm, very wet. And he can take the entire length of me into his throat, a pleasant fact that makes it possible to quite literally fuck his face. He finishes me and I finish him with my hand, and then we part, lightly patting each other's backs.

This is camaraderie, the group intimacy of gay men, a shared experience of lovemaking and passing, momentary affection. It is possible, as we know, to make love to the whole world.

Such late hours take their toll. At work, the next day, I am a zombie, going through the motions in a state of pure numbness. I have a killer headache, my back is sore from all the funny positions I was in, and my knees hurt (for obvious reasons). I vow never to stay out past one in the morning. No more coming home at half past three.

I go to Charlton's house to sit in his garden and drink iced tea. The garden is magnificent this year, his roses are spectacular, and pots are arranged haphazardly around the deck and the green garden beyond, pots of marigolds, impatiens, ranunculuses, and delicate, lavender alyssum. A lilac bush tumbles over the fence, blending with a fiery bougainvillea, giving way to dark green ivy. The fountain — a nude cherub peeing water out of his tiny penis — plashes and quite literally tinkles.

"You're lucky to have a real garden, a real back yard," I say, envying him. "We have nothing but three feet of a back porch, and the hill falls away precipitously beneath it."

"I love this garden," he says. "I only wish I had more time for it."

I wonder at this remark, because I know he has a Japanese gardener who tends the place twice a week — one of the luxuries of being wealthy, one of the necessities of having to be away for long periods of time, on press checks. I do not say anything about this.

Admiring the shrubs and flowers, and feeling at peace, I say, "It's heaven-sent, you know, sitting someplace so quiet, so restful. My house has been a battleground lately."

"They're not quarreling again, are they?" Charlton asks, a wry grin sneaking across his lips.

"Yes, they are, and it's much worse this time, because Scotty's had a slip-up of unprotected butt fucking."

"That boy! That idiot!" Charlton declares. "Whatever is he thinking of?"

"Oh, I don't know," I say. "I don't think it's so terribly shocking. If you think about, it's not very realistic to expect people to be perfectly safe, all the time, every time, over a period of fifteen, twenty years, or more. Things are bound to happen, condoms break—"

"But this was not a broken condom," Charlton pursues, "was it?"

"No," I answer, "it wasn't."

"Then what possible defense could Scotty have?"

"That the boy's dick was ten inches long and as big around as my forearm, hence a condom wouldn't fit it."

Charlton takes this in. He arches his eyebrows, "Well, if you're going to take a risk, I suppose it better be for something like that. That's the only thing that would make it worthwhile. But I don't buy this condom-doesn't-fit argument. I've heard it before. And I've never had any trouble, with any of my dates, some of whom have had quite large organs."

"Organs!" I laugh. "You sound like a medical conference. But I do buy the argument, because I've seen it happen myself. You know that from time to time I indulge a dusky taste, and many of the black men I've been with simply can't fit their dicks into those tiny condoms. When they try to stretch the condom to fit, the condom inevitably tears apart. What then are you supposed to do?"

"Don't get fucked," Charlton says, plainly, as though this conclusion should be painfully obvious.

"That's what I mean about being unrealistic," I say. "Passion, desire . . . they're all programmed into us. There's nothing wrong with wanting to have perfectly natural sex, without condoms. It's the most normal thing in the world. And it's an urge that's so basic, so biological, that it transcends even the most educated thoughts about risk. I hate to say it, but I always see infection as a matter of when, not if."

"That's a very pessimistic point of view," he says chidingly. "That supposes, or assumes, that everyone is going to let down their guard at some time in their sex life. I believe it's possible for people to remain safe, every time. I have!"

"But you're a finicky, prissy queen, Miss Hygiene herself. Look at your garden! There's not a blade of grass out of place or a single shriveled leaf."

"That's Ito's doing," he says, referring to the gardener. I smile to myself.

And then I remember his cancer checkup, appalled that I've forgotten it entirely. I hasten to ask, "How'd your doctor's visit go?"

"I was wondering when you'd ask," he says. "Not all the tests are in yet, but the preliminary report is that I'm fine, still cancer free."

"That's great," I say, genuinely enthusiastic. At least one person, I think, has some good news. But I don't say this, feeling, at the moment, that I don't want to invite a discussion about the miseries of life. Surely I don't need that now, these days.

But then Charlton takes a long sip of the mineral water, and, staring at a clump of late-blooming gladiolas, asks, "How is your work with Emma going?"

For a moment I am lost. Emma? Emma who? And then I realize that he is asking about Dr. Kiljoy. "Oh, fine," I say, quietly.

"That doesn't sound very enthusiastic."

"No, I don't mean to sound . . . whatever . . . But I still have my doubts about therapy. We've been talking a lot about man stuff, what it means to be a man and all that—"

"Oh, Christ!" Charlton cuts in. "Get over it, Mary."

"Well, no, it's important stuff," I go on. "I'm trying to figure out how to be an adult. That's something you of all people should be interested in."

This remark is met with silence, but not a hostile silence. Just expectancy.

"But as for the depression stuff," I continue, "there's been some improvement, mainly I think because of the antidepressant, not because of the therapy—"

"But it was therapy that got you to the shrink to get the pills," Charlton says, conclusively.

"That's true enough. I guess," I say. "The problem is, I want to be a different person, someone grown up, someone who is able, gracefully, to leave childhood and boyhood behind and move easily into whatever's next."

"And you don't see that talk therapy can do that for you, do you?"

"No, I don't," I tell him. "I don't see it at all. I've been over this stuff with other therapists, and it goes nowhere. I thought, for some reason, that Dr. Kiljoy would be different. But I'm beginning to suspect that psychotherapy in general just isn't very effective."

"Oh, I don't know if I'd say that," Charlton muses. "If anything, you're already defining the problems, starting to come to grips with them, and most importantly starting to formulate a picture in your mind of who you want to be. That's what therapy is all about."

"But how can I change?" I ask (somewhat desperately).

Charlton is quiet for a moment, looking down into his lap. Then he lights another cigarette and asks, "Have you ever considered pursuing a spiritual solution to these problems, these issues of yours?"

"A what?"

"A spiritual solution," he says. "When I had cancer, it wasn't any particular thing that pulled me through, it was a combination of many different things — conventional medical therapy — chemo — and macrobiotics, therapy, and spirituality. It's a holistic approach—"

"I know about holism," I say. "Remember, I edit for a New Age publisher."

"But have you ever put any of it into practice?"

"God, you sound like an AA meeting!"

"So what?" Charlton shrugs. "If it worked for me, why not try it for yourself. The worst thing that can happen is that nothing will come of it. Big deal."

"But it's so damned ridiculous, praying and meditating and all that nonsense. I've been through all that when I got clean and sober—"

"And didn't it work then?" he asks.

"Well, yes, in a way," I admit. Grudgingly, I think, it did work very well, for a number of years. I just drifted away from it all, became disillusioned. But I'll be damned if I'm going to take up that whole business again.

"I suppose I could try," I say. In a pig's eye, I tell myself, silently.

"I'm not talking about anything silly, I'm talking about reawakening the spiritual part of yourself, to let you expand and breathe and get to the person you want to be. That's all."

I greet this with another silence, this California talk. I reach for another cigarette, a nervous habit when I'm uncomfortable, which I am now. Yes, I know this stuff works, but I resent it, because it seems silly.

"Well, think about it," Charlton concludes. "You don't have to do anything you don't want to."

Changing the subject, I say (disconnectedly): "Speaking of sex, how's what's-his-name, Derek?"

"Oh, her."

"Oh, that bad, huh?"

"Well, no, he's great . . . well, not great . . . he's just somehow not . . . cooperative."

"In what way?" I urge.

"He doesn't want to go to movies, he doesn't want to go to the opera, he's not much interested in travel. But he is good sex."

"Perhaps he just has other interests?" I suggest.

"Yes, indeed, interests in snorting speed and dancing all night long." Charlton sighs. "I'm too old for all of that."

"I suppose," I venture, "that that's one of the drawbacks of dating someone from a younger generation, the disparity in energy levels, in interests."

Charlton grunts at this last offer. "No, I don't think that's it. He's just got his own world, and he's not interested in going any farther. He just wants to 'party and play,' as he says. Repeatedly."

"But that's a truly tired scene," I agree, and then continue, "How long is this sort of thing going to go on? This drug stuff and this dancing stuff and all this body worship and just plain nonsense? Are gay guys ever going to grow up?"

"That's a fine remark coming from you, Miss Musclething, Miss Gym Bunny—"

"Gym Rat," I correct him. "I'm too old to be a bunny, of any sort."

"Whatever," he sighs. "I just don't know what to do anymore. I have so few contemporaries left. Most everyone's been claimed by the plague. One has no choice but to seek thrills in another generation."

"How about someone older?" I suggest.

To this, he pauses, then sighs again. "No, no, I'm old enough as it is. I'm fifty for Chrissake. Someone older would be . . . well . . . pushing it."

"So you, too, are a victim of the adoration of youth," I conclude.

Charlton rolls his eyes. "Have another cigarette, you need one."

We both light up and sit in silence, staring into the garden, into the deep shadows behind the fountain. It's almost a grotto, I expect to see a vision of the Virgin any moment.

Finally, easing himself out of his chair, Charlton takes, rather absent-mindedly, a pair of garden shears and begins to clip roses. "Here, take some of these home with you," he commands, handing me a bundle of yellow, red, and dazzling white roses.

I accept them and understand that he is dismissing me. Fine, I think, this conversation has become a bore. These issues, these problems — always seem irresolvable. Youth, aging, relationships, matters of the heart. Why must they be eternally difficult?

◆

Apparently, Scotty has told Kent about his bareback experience, and the aftermath has proven quite gruesome. The arguing, the silence, the stomping, slamming doors, and disappearance of one or the other of them from the apartment — it's all unsettling. I hate this part of living with a couple. Fight and fuck, that's what couples do. (Oh, but how can I be so cynical?)

After two days of this nonsense, Kent has agreed to go with Scotty to be tested, again, together. It's been a year since they both tested negative, so I suppose it's time for them to recheck. It would be disastrous — tragic — if Scotty were to test positive and Kent, too, because that would mean that, indeed, Scotty had infected Kent (if Kent's profession of utter fidelity is in fact true; one can never really know).

◆

I am at Anson's house, watching movies on video. First we watch *Taxi Driver* (he has never before seen it) and then *Interview with the Vampire*, which whets our appetites for the gothic. "Perhaps we should go to that new goth club next weekend, what is it called?" I remark, casually.

"Black Death," Anson answers, and then pursues the thought: "We could go for drinks at the Hole in the Wall and then move on to Black Death when it's late enough."

"You know, that's one thing I've always hated about San Francisco," I remark, "how late the club scene is."

"Oh, but it's not!" Anson says, emphatically. "Compared to New York, or even L.A., San Francisco is an early city. There's hardly a restaurant or club open past two or three."

"Doesn't Universe last till something like six or seven in the morning?"

"Yes," he answers, "but you have to be a lot younger than we are to do that. And besides, we're clean. I don't think anyone can dance all night, till dawn, without doing a bump or two."

"Ugh," I groan. "I cannot abide tweakers. They're completely useless. Their mouths are dry, their sweat smells funny, and they can't hold still long enough for a good fuck. And to top it all off, they can't keep a hardon!"

"Hopeless!" Anson agrees. "But I used to do it, when I was in my twenties."

"And so did I," I say. "Cocaine was big in those days, the early eighties, and the speed was heaven. I could go for hours and hours, dancing and then going to the baths. It seems a world of time away."

"It is," Anson agrees. "Can you imagine that we came to adulthood in the era of *Dynasty* and *Dallas*?"

"I don't know that I would use the word adulthood, not to describe my early twenties. At that age, you're really still something of an adolescent. At least I think so."

"I'd have to agree," he says. He sighs. He stares off into space.

I wonder what he's thinking. But I don't ask, because I really don't want to know. This is the first relationship I've ever had where the past didn't matter very much, the first where the important thing is the present moment, the now of it all, the way we treat each other. Isn't that what matters, in the end?

He stands and walks into the kitchen. I hear him rummaging in the refrigerator. He brings me a glass of lemonade and leans over me, massaging my neck and shoulders.

"Hmmm, that feels marvelous," I say (meaning let's fuck).

"I'll bet it does," he says (meaning yes, let's).

"Do you remember much about the days before safe sex? Before condoms?" he asks.

"Yes, I do, as a matter of fact." I remember way too much, I think, incredulous that there was a time when contagion was nothing to worry about. All the social diseases were curable.

"I don't," he says. "I know my first sexual experiences were right at the time the epidemic was breaking, but I was so young, so naive. I didn't think, back in Georgia, that it had anything to do with me." He is silent then, a silence that bespeaks envy, wistfulness.

"Those were crazy times," I say, "looking back on it now. Do you remember, in *And the Band Played On*, when Randy Shilts writes about Selma Dritz's public health concerns, when she pointed to a graph depicting the rise in various STDs and said, 'Too much is being transmitted here.' Do you remember that?"

"Oh, yes, I do remember," he says. "When I read that, I shuddered. I had a chill. I read that when I had just arrived in the City."

Both of us are silent, again, letting our thoughts expand and contract. Actually, I don't have any thoughts at the moment, except for the idea of getting him into bed for some hot, sweaty sex.

We go into the bedroom and fall atop the sheets, all hands and sucking and desire. We get rougher and rougher, going at it like rapists (not really). He submits, I submit. We take turns.

We sleep the night through, waking at half past eight. I will be late for work, he will be late for class.

Unbidden, as I prepare for work, the question posed in the recent conversation with Charlton reforms itself in my mind. Why must matters of the heart be so complicated?

But I can not justify this thought, not now. Nothing has gone wrong. The evening, and night, with Anson have been wonderful, a dream almost.

And then I see it, the idea that this relationship is something of a dream. For a moment, a fleeting moment in which I feel an enormous panic rise and fall, I understand that I don't really know Anson. I know only the role that I've wanted Anson to fill.

Too troubling, this thought. I banish it as I scrub my teeth clean, digging the bristles into my gums until they bleed. The admonishment of my dentist rings in my ears, "Healthy gums do not bleed."

And at this thought, I imagine that I'm going crazy, truly nuts. The world and everything in it is completely out of place, ragged, unstoppable, wicked.

11

Autumn — with its brilliant blue skies, cotton candy clouds, the lingering scent of firewood in the morning air, the gentle, warm rains, and the occasional cold breeze from the north — has fully arrived in San Francisco. I am lying on the rooftop of my building, taking the September sun. In the distance I can see the inner bay, beyond China Basin, below the Bay Bridge. Tiny white triangles of sailboats dart about the emerald, bluish waters of the bay. The bridge shimmers in the glaring sunlight. The feel of the city is slow, lethargic, everyone slain by the heat.

Walking up Castro Street on the way to my appointment with Dr. Kiljoy, I encounter the same cute, homeless punkboy begging for money that I saw a couple weeks ago. I reach into my pocket and finger the change, then decide to pull out a dollar and give it to him. He's so cute. This time, I don't feel guilty.

But where do all these beggars, these so-called homeless people come from? It's a puzzle to me, and every time the papers run a story about the homeless, I scan the story, trying to understand what's happened in these people's lives that's driven them into the streets. Have they no family, no friends, no one to whom they can turn for help? This seems (to my middle-class comfortable self) incomprehensible.

And then, of course, there are the nuts, the clearly insane people, their brains fried on drugs or twisted by mental illness, wandering the streets, unable to care for themselves, begging spare change, muttering and shouting inanities. I wonder, what kind of society are we that we can't help these folks?

But then I reach the Duboce Triangle, with its tall, shady trees, its quaint narrow streets, its compact Victorians and Edwardians. I wonder, as I mount the stairs to Dr. Kiljoy's office, what will we discuss today?

The usual small talk out of the way, Dr. Kiljoy fixes her eye on me and asks, "How are you feeling?"

"Okay, I guess. Not much to report," I tell her. "The antidepressant is beginning to work. I thought you'd want to know that."

"How are you feeling about the medication?"

"Fine, happy, glad that I'm taking it," I answer. "If I'd known it was this easy to feel a little better, I'd have done it a long time ago."

"That's the tricky thing about depression," she says. "One never fully grasps that one is in its grip. All is darkness and gloom, it seems as though the world is underwater somehow, that nothing can ever be right. It seems to be reality—"

"But it's not," I finish for her. "But does this new-found cheeriness mean that I am merely drugged in the other direction, lifted up beyond reality onto a plane of giddiness?"

"Do you feel giddy? Do you feel unreal? Do you feel as though you are intoxicated, not in control?"

"No, no, I don't feel that way," I say. Wistfully, I look past her, to the windows, and muse, "Autumn is a wonderful time of the year, isn't it?"

She nods, a slight frown creasing her brow, betraying puzzlement at my sudden, out-of-place remark. "Yes, it's a lovely season," she agrees (somewhat reluctantly).

And then I wonder, am I wasting my time? Isn't the antidepressant enough? Could it be that I should save my money and end all this talking, all this speculation? But no, I answer myself, these discussion of manhood — adulthood — are proving helpful (revealing, empowering). I think of Charlton and wonder if he's right, I need to do everything to take care of myself, including this form of support, this therapy, this inward analysis and personal inventory. And there sits Dr. Kiljoy, regarding me with her dark, sultry brown eyes, awaiting some word, some opening issue.

"Yes, I do love autumn," I say, repeating myself. Then, while I'm thinking I should quit all this, it is indeed a waste of time, a waste of money, she says:

"Last week, at the end of the hour, you were saying that you feel that therapy is not enough, that you're seeking transformation — I think that's the word you used — that you want to be somebody else."

Has she just read my mind?

"Can you tell me more about that, elaborate a bit?"

"Uh . . . sure . . ." I stumble. "Well . . . let me see . . . it's a big question for me, one that keeps coming up, in my mind, just about every day. I was talking to Charlton about this a couple of days ago, and of all things, he suggested to me that my problem is really a spiritual problem, not depression—"

"Depression can be a spiritual problem," she says, quietly. Her voice, I notice, is low, whispery. And perhaps, I detect, a touch annoyed. Why annoyance?

"Well, yes, then . . ." I'm momentarily at a loss. And then, "I guess I'm not really sure anymore what spirituality is. What is it?"

"You're asking me?" she says. "You want my definition?"

I nod.

"One simple way I have always put it, is to think about the other dimensions of life — think about the physical, the body, the brain, your organ systems, metabolism, neurotransmitters, the whole thing. Then think about your mind, psychology, consciousness, awareness, cognition, thinking and behavior patterns, the ego. Now consider your emotions, your feelings, moods, disposition, passion, love, anger, hurt. When you've recognized all those, then whatever's left is your spirituality."

"My word!" I declare, completely taken aback with her dryness, with this definition. But is there truth to what she says?

"Consider a very simple phrase we all use, all the time — the spirit of things. The spirit of the times, the spirit of the party, the life of the party, the spirit of the nation. It is something that touches the emotional, the psychological, and the physical but is beyond them, clearly outside these rather plain, everyday things."

Ah, she's making more sense. And I realize that of course, I know what spirituality is. Of course I understand the concept, this otherness, this outside dimension.

"I think what Charlton is trying to tell you is that without bringing the spiritual into play, there can be no lasting change, no real transformation," she concludes.

"This is fine and dandy," I venture, "it all sounds good, but it also sounds simple, too easy. And yet . . . how . . . how does a person get their spirit to transform them?"

"A good question," she says, a tad condescendingly for my tastes. But she goes on, "That is the question at the heart of all spiritual traditions, all holy quests, all religions. Transformation, both in this life and in the life beyond, if you believe in that."

"So I'm in good company?" I ask, rather meekly.

"Indeed," she answers.

"But what do I want to transform? I still don't know!"

"To repeat myself, that is why we are here. That is our challenge. There seems no other work we need to do more than this," she says, with great authority.

I accept this authority, because it feels right to have her speak more declaratively. I sense she is able to be even more blunt but is holding back.

"I think you could be more direct with me," I say, in a tone of admonishment.

"All right," she says. "Last week you said that you want to be someone else. But I don't think you mean that you want to be another person, a separate entity. I think you want to be a new, improved version of yourself, and I think that what you want is to learn to be a man."

Ugh, the manhood thing again. I say, "God, how I resist that word, that concept. Whenever we talk about manhood, I feel like a traitor, betraying all my feminist sisters or something, turning the clock back, trying to become some kind of macho butch hulk—"

"But 'macho' and 'butch' are not the same as manhood and masculinity," she observes.

This stops me dead in the water. What?

Noting my muteness, she goes on: "You're equating the trappings of manliness with being a man, with masculine qualities. They are not the same thing. Big muscles or lumberjack clothes do not make a man. If that were the case, we'd have many lesbian men walking around town."

"But we do, we do," I say, laughing.

"No, butch is not manhood," she says, ignoring my attempted levity.

I ask: "But isn't butch — physical strength, overt masculinity, trucks and boots — symbolic of masculinity? Aren't they the manifestation of manhood?"

"No, they are not," she says, simply and softly. She's taken on a very demure, almost feminine attitude suddenly. And then I realize that of course, she's going to display her femininity in counterpoint to our discussion of masculinity. How very clever of her!

"Think about masculinity," she pursues. "What qualities do you see as being masculine?"

"Well, there's strength and toughness, looking like—"

"No, not toughness, and not looking like anything. That is macho, machismo, butchness. I want to know what qualities you associate with being masculine."

She's got me there. My mind is a blank. I say nothing. I cross my legs. She crosses her legs, adopting a mirrored position of my own. In body language, I muse to myself, this is called sympathetic posturing.

"All right," she begins again. "What literary or film figures do you revere as masculine. And why?"

Instantly I answer, "James Bond."

"And why?" she urges.

"Because he is suave and coolheaded, even in a crisis, always strong, always dependable, a womanizing ravisher," I say.

"Suave, womanizing — we can dispense with those, that's macho stuff. But you're onto something with strong, dependable, coolheaded."

I go on: "There's the character of Jack Ryan, in Tom Clancy's novels. I've always thought of him as being a really wonderful man. And Morgan Freeman, in the roles he plays. And Colin Powell . . . Oh! I can't believe I said that!"

"Why not?" she asks.

"Because, obviously, we're not supposed to admire Colin Powell, not at all. He opposed gays in the military, he's a right-wing Republican, he's associated with Reagan, and Bush, and just everything that's—"

"That's what?" she cuts in.

"That's wrong about how things are!"

"Then why did he come to mind as representative of masculinity?" she asks.

"Because I read his autobiography," I tell her (honestly). "And I was impressed that, even though I couldn't agree with many of his beliefs, I admired that he tried, always, to find the balance point in things. He's not an intolerant man, as the discussions in the gay community might suggest. He tries to be fair. He tries to do the right thing. Or at least the thing that he believes to be right."

"And that," she declares, "is the essence of being a man."

God, this is distressing me. Colin Powell? Jack Ryan? James Bond? Morgan Freeman? Why Morgan Freeman? I ask myself. And answer, because, in the film *Seven*, he remarks, sarcastically, to Brad Pitt that it's "impressive to see a man feeding on his emotions." And he means impressive in the sense that it's striking, not that it's admirable. And this spoke volumes to me about how our culture holds emotions in such high regard, as though they are the be-all and end-all of life. I believe that emotions are highly overrated. And I do not want to feed off them, do not want to be enslaved by them. Is that something else that being a man is about?

I say none of this to Dr. Kiljoy. I am embarrassed enough as it is.

"Could we examine this a bit more closely now?" she requests. "What qualities do these men share that you admire?"

"Well, there's the old thing about the strong, silent type. But isn't that the rigid, unfeeling mess of manhood that our fathers all followed?"

"Strength, and quietude are admirable, masculine traits. It's the coolheadedness that you mentioned before."

"All right," I go on, "there's a sense of protectiveness, of watching out for others, that comes, in part, I think, from men's physical strength, that they're able to physically defend, or protect, others who are being threatened."

She nods and winces a small smile.

"And then there's the thing about fatherhood," and here I falter. "I don't mean being a father in the biological sense. I could be a father if I found the right lesbian and turkey baster." I laugh, but Dr. Kiljoy doesn't respond.

"What I mean about fatherhood is that sense of nurturing . . . no . . . I mean . . . well, yes, nurturing and of moral strength . . . more along the lines of moral leadership, of being a provider."

She nods again. I see that I'm digging out what she wants me to get at. This is fun.

"And I guess I'd value honesty in a man, but then I'd value honesty in a woman. Maybe I mean something more like frankness."

I stop then, exhausted from the effort of reaching within. She makes that funny shift in her chair, tugging at the skirt of her suit to keep it from riding up. She smoothes her lap with her hands, then clasps them together. I observe: how psychotherapeutic!

"We're running short on time," she states. "We have a few more minutes. Is there anything else?"

I search my mind, finding a nugget. "Well, speaking of man things, I went out this weekend, to a sex club, and was wildly sexual with a number of anonymous guys . . . oh, god, I sound like an STD counselor . . . it was one of those times I call 'long nights and sweet strangers.' I had a very good time, but when I got home, I felt strangely, that I'd somehow betrayed Anson. Isn't that a ridiculous thing to feel?

"Of course I dismissed it at once. I'll have no notions of fidelity or restrictions placed on me — that's where I agree with Scotty. But as lacking as I felt the experience was in terms of intimacy, real heartfelt intimacy, it was rich in adventure. It seems to be, as Scotty has said, a 'man thing', this going out hunting for conquests, some kind of a primordial urge to go out hunting, to see what I can get. It makes me wonder, how can I find that in the context of a relationship?"

I shut up then, because I recognize that I am beginning to psychobabble. Time to zip it up.

"Well, we can talk more about that next week, if you like," she says. "But our time is up."

And after she hands me her bill for services, I hasten down the stairs and out into the brilliant, blinding glare of autumn light.

12

Anson and I meet after work (and after school, for him) at Peet's. We order plain black coffee and share a dry stale scone. We debate where to go for dinner and settle, finally, on the Firewood. Anson loves pasta with four-cheese sauce. We stroll up Eighteenth, hand in hand, no wind tonight, the air still and warm. The last week of September.

At dinner, trying to relate my day at the office, I fear I am making a jumbled mess of a bad situation (one of the assistant editors has promised an author a contract, quite out of her power to do so, and I am attempting to correct the situation, protect the firm from a lawsuit). Anson chews his food and looks at me, or rather, I think, past me. Clearly he couldn't care less about my work troubles.

Annoyed, gearing for an argument, I feel suddenly hostile, hurtful. What can I say? Should I say You're not paying attention to me? Or should I clam up and say nothing more, let him figure out that I'm upset about something?

I do neither, letting my story tumble to its inevitable, speculative conclusion (that the author will graciously understand and withdraw her manuscript).

But I am saddened, during this simple dinner, in this plain restaurant with its long polished wooden tables, the autumn light fading beyond the windows to a deep, luscious indigo. For this is the first time I have felt annoyed with Anson. But such a thing is inevitable, I tell myself. Let it go. Don't harbor a resentment over something so silly. Perhaps he's preoccupied with an upcoming exam? Maybe he's just tired?

Whatever, I swallow my irritation and shut up. This seems to relieve Anson. He begins to tell me of his day, of his week. "One of my professors is a total asshole," he's saying to me. "And he seems to have singled me out for special treatment — special being calling on me endlessly, hoping, I think, that I'll have the wrong answer or no answer at all."

My annoyance flares again. I am bored, he is boring me. Again, I'm saddened by this first experience, with Anson, of these temperamental feelings. But isn't this normal? Isn't this inevitable? Things can't be rosy all the time, I tell myself. If I learn right now, here, to choose gentleness over anger and boredom, I'll be better off in the long run.

After dinner we return to my flat and lay down, which (amazingly, given my recent annoyance) turns to a wild steamy hot session of fucking and sucking.

Afterwards, my tensions dissolved, we are ready to go out for the evening. We stop at the Hole in the Wall for a drink. It is the usual collection of misfits, freaks, potheads, dinosaur punks, and queers, even some old-style leathermen and mustachioed gays. Alien Sex Fiend is playing in the background, ". . . now I'm feeling zombified, now I'm feeling zombified . . ." And I think, but do not say: Precisely.

But truly, I don't feel like a zombie, not at all. Sex, lovemaking, intimacy, all the things Anson and I have just done, have elevated my mood considerably. And I am, once again, restored to an enthusiastic, natural high.

We go on to Black Death, where they are playing Siouxie and the Banshees, Butthole Surfers, 45 Grave, Bauhaus. Clumps of thin pale black-enshrouded death rockers drift around the club, smoking heavily, swaying to the music. It is, as Anson says, "just like Halloween."

We get drinks — mineral water for me (for my struggling sobriety) and beer for Anson — and drift about the space, a vast dark warehouse, open, vaulted with steel beams peppered with banks of colored lights, lasers, and strobes. This space, this cavernous warehouse, is home to many clubs. Black Death is just one of six nightly gatherings, ruling Sunday nights. Saturdays are held by club Surgery, which caters to punk rockers, queers, and fetish freaks and features a variety of blood-letting acts on the elevated stage. Tuesdays are Mamba, a Latino club; Wednesday's are club August, a perpetual beach party for retro-yuppies, and Thursdays and Fridays are dedicated to plain old disco, including, of course, the spinning disco ball casting dots of lights in a dizzying circle.

These facts we ascertain by examining the bulletin board of the place, because, quite frankly, we don't know what to do with ourselves. We had thought to get "in touch with" our mutual goth "roots," but after only a half hour, we are bored.

"Let's go to the Exchange," Anson suggests. "Maybe we can get into trouble there."

Without hesitation, we depart and drive through SOMA to the club, another vast dark multi-level warehouse. The crowd is youngish, very cute, quite muscled, and faintly, strangely sleazy. Perfect.

We stroll about the place, studying various couplings, threesomes, foursomes, whatever-somes. Finally, we attract a smooth short and very cute boy, a little goatee sprouting from his chin. He is what we would call a boy toy (or a toy boy), and that is exactly what we do with him — toy with him — this way and that, up and down, front and back, until every possible combination and position — and nearly every possible sex act — have been done.

The boy vanishes when we are finished, fading into the darkness. We never asked his name, nor he ours. Anson and I clean up and go out, entering the cool foggy night. Strange, I comment, to see fog in autumn.

The next day, I call Michael, inquiring after his new program of acupuncture and Chinese herbs.

"It's going amazingly well," he tells me, breathlessly. "I already feel worlds better, and it's only been a couple of weeks. I wish I'd done this a long time ago."

I think but do not say: Well, we tried and tried to get you to do something, anything, but you were a stubborn asshole.

" . . . so I feel some renewal, even hope . . . I might even give those brand new drugs a try. I called the doctor, and he said that yes, I might be able to tolerate them. And I checked with the Chinese doctor, and he didn't think it would hurt anything, so long as I kept up my herbal regimen and drink a lot of water. He's big on water. Oh, and he wants me to meditate. He's also very big on meditation. But I'm not so sure about that, after all—"

"How's Mama Jones?" I cut in, as she suddenly pops to mind.

"Oh!" Michael exclaims. Which puts me ill at ease. Something in his tone is worrying. "She went to the women's clinic and they didn't really find anything, nothing particularly overt, but they could see, and tell from her description, that something is most definitely, seriously wrong. So she managed to get an appointment with her regular doctor — a small miracle, she could see Mama the very next day due to a cancellation — and the upshot of all this is that Mama is checking into Presbyterian Hospital at the end of the week for a complete workup."

Now I say, "Oh." Trying to think what to say next — because I don't want to upset Michael, who so depends on Mama — I hesitate, drawing out the word "well" for some time. Then: "It must be something serious." Not wanting to alarm Michael, I next contradict myself.

"But it's probably nothing, really. Just something like mono," I offer.

"Let's hope so," Michael agrees. "I have to say that I'm glad to be doing a little better myself, because I don't know what I would do if I were sicker, with Mama in the hospital and all."

"Don't be silly," I say. "Of course we would all take care of you." Which reminds me that, with Mama in the hospital, perhaps Thomas will take over Michael's care. And so I ask, "Do you need more help, I mean, when she's in the hospital? Or are you feeling well enough yourself? Can Thomas step in? Does he have the time?"

Slightly exasperated, Michael says, "I just told you that I'll be fine, because I don't need much care, not now at least, really."

Our conversation is crumbling, as I fumble yet again. "Well, please call me if you need . . . well, you know, I guess Thomas will be okay . . ."

"What are you trying to say?"

"Just that . . . that . . . oh, hell, I'm just worried sick over Mama. I have this bad feeling."

"Like a premonition?" Michael suggests.

"Yes, I'm afraid so," I say. And then sigh. "Let's hope it's not woman's intuition."

"Yes, let's hope," Michael says. "I've got to go boil my herbs now. God, you wouldn't believe how they stink up the place. Ghastly. And they don't taste any better than they smell. But I guess it's worth it."

And Michael hangs up.

In the days that follow, Michael again takes a sharp and sudden downward turn. It seems more than I, or any of us, can bear, with Mama in the hospital being tested for god-knows-what. I stop by Michael and Thomas's flat without calling.

Thomas buzzes me in, and as I reach the top of the stairs, where I can look directly into their bedroom, I see Michael half sitting up in bed, half slouched over. He's very pale, ashen really, and his ears seem to stick out of his head. I realize this is because he's lost even more weight, in just a matter of days.

Thomas motions me down the hall. "Michael is actually snoozing," he tells me, "though he looks half awake. When he sleeps these days, his eyes are slightly open. The doctor told me that wasn't a good sign."

"Oh," I quietly say. "What can I do?"

"Nothing, nothing really," Thomas answers. "Mama is due back next week, Monday or Tuesday. I just hope Michael's downturn doesn't affect her health."

All of a sudden I blurt out: "But how are you holding up? What are we going to do? Should we organize a team effort, all take turns helping out? I mean, well . . ." Surprisingly (or not surprisingly, really) I am on the verge of tears, a rarity for me. I try to examine the cause, but Thomas is talking. I listen.

"No, there's no need for that now. I've got things under control. And we just have to see about Mama, how much care she'll need, if any. They're giving her intravenous saline, you know, to hydrate her, and she actually looked a little better when I stopped by yesterday, less drawn. Intravenous hydration does wonders for your skin."

He says this in a queeny voice. "The beauty treatment of the new millennium," I say.

Thomas, as always, is exhibiting tremendous, amazing strength. I know I didn't hold up so well when my lovers were sick. He simply does what's needed, whatever's next. "What's the next right thing?" he often asks himself, in a whisper. I recognize this, as it's a question I learned in AA many years ago. I'd forgotten that Thomas, too, is clean and sober.

My conversations with Dr. Kiljoy come to mind, when I think about Thomas. He is one of those "real" men, a solid, masculine pillar of strength. He is certainly the epitome of the strong, silent type. I admire this. But I wonder, does he ever lose it, just go nuts, break down and cry or something? It's hard to imagine Thomas in tears, but it wouldn't be a shock to me. My admiration would undoubtedly grow, to see a man who knew the right time and the right moment to shed his tears of grief, of impending loss.

Thinking about Thomas, in this way, I find him very attractive. For a moment, I think of sex with Thomas, as though I could somehow absorb his masculine strength by taking him into myself. And in the next moment, I think that, when Michael dies, perhaps I can have a fling with Thomas. But I banish the thought at once. What a horrible thing to think! And what about Anson?

When Scotty and Kent go for their test results, they are both dismayed by the results. Kent is negative. Scotty tests positive.

Stunned, that evening, they are mostly quiet. I don't know what's happened until Scotty finally takes me aside, in the pantry, and tells me the news.

"Good god," I say. And then I can't say another word. I'm neither surprised nor shocked. I feel nothing.

"It was really very funny, in a way," Scotty's telling me. "The counselor just started her job this week, and I was the first person she had to deliver the news to about seroconverting. She was in tears, and Kent and I ended up consoling *her*."

I try to laugh, but this doesn't strike me as funny. Strange, I tell myself, I should be grief-stricken, concerned, aghast at this staggering news. But I am not. This must be some sort of state of shock, I tell myself. It will catch up with me eventually, I'm sure. Bad news always does.

Composing myself, I ask, "But how is Kent taking this? He must be furious."

"I think he is, underneath. But I don't think he's aware of it yet. At the moment, he's acting very solicitous and playing concerned. I'm not very upset, I guess I should be, but I'm not, it's not unexpected, after all the things I've been doing all these years, but I'm a little upset that it's probably the two times I've been barebacked, *not* all the years of sucking dick. I'm not sure it was worth it, even though I'm not worrying about it at all, you know . . ."

"Well," I say, "let's give him some space and see how it goes. Are you going to see the doctor now? Start antivirals?"

"I don't know," he answers, "I don't know what to do at this point."

Later, after supper, waiting for Anson to come over, I sit in my room, perched on the edge of my bed, and the tears start coming, hot anguished tears. It's always like this when I finally do cry, years and years of pent-up grief disposing itself in wrenching sobs, which I attempt to silence. I don't like to cry, it reminds me of my crazy aunt, who would burst into tears over absolutely nothing.

◆

In the midst of all this turmoil, Anson is my source of strength. And later that evening, I wail, "How can this be? Everything around me is falling apart. And it's not the first time. It's the umpteenth time. I wonder when I'm going to run out of patience, when I'm not going to be able to cope anymore. When I'm going to have to take a drive halfway across the Golden Gate Bridge. I feel like Louise Lasser in *Mary Hartman, Mary Hartman*, my world imploding."

Anson says, "Then I must be Mary Kay Place."

13

The morning of my next therapy session is a bright shimmering fall day: October. No clouds, no fog, just warm glowing light. I rise early and follow my morning rituals: hot tea, cereal, the newspaper, a cigarette. Stretching, shaving, showering, dressing. On my way to the office, I realize that it's going to be a scorching day. I've overdressed.

The morning flies by, buried, as I am, in a lengthy manuscript about Buddhism. At lunch, at home, I change into comfortable, summery clothes, shorts and a loose T-shirt. The afternoon free, except for therapy, I walk through the Castro in a roundabout way, stopping at the bookstore to examine new titles, having a small dish of chocolate ice cream, reading the headlines of *The New York Times* that someone has left on the counter of the ice cream shop.

Thus fortified, I'm ready to face Dr. Kiljoy, and face the overwhelming circumstances of my life.

"And how has your week been?" she asks, standing at the windows, drawing back the heavy drapes and opening the windows as far as they will go.

"Terrible, just terrible," I tell her. "It's been an awful week, too much going on, too many things to absorb at the same time . . . I don't really know where to begin—"

"Last week, we discussed more about masculinity, about what it means to be a man—"

"I don't want to talk about that, at least not today. Maybe not anymore. There's too much that's happening in my life for me to spend my energy analyzing these abstractions."

She lowers her chin and purses her lips. I guess I've been a bit abrupt.

"Sorry," I say, "I don't mean to be curt, but really, too many things are happening."

"Such as?" she prompts.

"Such as Scotty's HIV test came back positive, Mama Jones is in the hospital, Michael, after a sudden upswing, is failing again. Anson annoys me . . . but oh, he's wonderful, the only bright spot in my life right now. I don't know how I could be annoyed with him."

"What is he doing that annoys you?" she asks.

"Oh, nothing, really," I answer. "It's just that at dinner the other night, I felt irritated that he wasn't paying attention to what I was saying. The important part, the part that bothered me, was that that's the first time I've felt irritation with Anson. It seemed to color things a different shade—"

"Made him more real?" she suggests.

"Yes, exactly, and that's the kind of thing that's been happening, Anson is becoming more real. I think we talked about this before, that I felt like I had an ideal image in my mind of what I wanted in a boyfriend, and that he's filling that image, that job almost, very well. But as I move deeper into a relationship with him, I'm finding that that objectification is falling away, and I'm confronted with a real human being, another man, someone who sometimes snores in his sleep, who can ignore me at times, who drinks too much water with meals. Little things, I know, but grating. It's been a long time since I've had to adjust like this, in this way."

"It's perfectly understandable," she says, in a soothing way. "We all have our little faults — at least in the eyes of others — and learning to be close to someone takes time. One has to allow for these sorts of things. One has to be prepared for conflict, too, because it is inevitable that you will quarrel, about something, sometimes. Don't be taken by surprise, and don't react in a childish way."

"Easier said than done, I'll bet." As soon as I say this, I regret the cliché.

The noise of construction floods through the open windows — hammers pounding, voices shouting instructions, saws screaming.

"There's something else, too, that's bothering me, and Scotty's seroconversion has something to do with it."

I'm silent for a moment.

"And that is . . . ?" she prompts.

"Well, the other night, we went out to a sex club and had a great time with this cute little guy. And it was . . . was . . . a lot of fun, almost more fun than sex with Anson alone. But different, very different, because, even though Anson was there, playing with us, there wasn't the passion I usually feel with Anson. But when we fuck at home, it's wildly passionate. Feelings of love, ecstasy, transcendence . . . Oh, I don't know what I'm getting at."

"You're talking about the difference between recreational sex and emotional, passionate intimacy," she tells me " . . . the difference between having sex and making love. They are different things."

I shake my head, wondering what I'm trying to get at, and failing to grasp it. "Yes, yes, I know all that. I've always been very clear about that. But somehow, with Scotty getting infected in the midst of turmoil with Kent about monogamy versus an open relationship, somehow I've got a twinge of something . . ." I falter, unsure where I'm heading. " . . . something I've never felt before, as if I want to be monogamous with Anson, shut out any recreational sex, focus all my energies on just the two of us."

"And you find that disturbing?" she asks.

"Yes, I do," I answer, "because I've always, always had my head screwed on right, knowing, believing, that monogamy is about control, about a power struggle in a relationship . . ."

"And now you're seeing things somewhat differently?" she probes.

"Yes." I take a deep breath before going on. "I'm surprised at myself, and I'm surprised that in all these years, as adamantly opposed to monogamy as I've been, I've never considered the possibility . . . this possibility . . . of monogamy as a way to build the energy between two people. Oh, I know that sounds kind of superstitious, talking about 'energy' between us. But what I mean is, by focusing on

Anson, and only Anson, by making love with only Anson, and having sex with only him, we might grow even closer."

"Do you find that frightening?" she asks.

"I'm not sure fear is what I feel . . ." I stop for a moment, considering my feelings and pondering what to say next. And then: "But perhaps that's right. I'm afraid of being on new ground, of wanting something I've always been opposed to. It's the crumbling of a core belief I've always held. That frightens me, and annoys me, and makes me wonder just what other things in my head are stubborn or misguided."

"Have you discussed this with Anson?" she asks.

"No, we haven't discussed anything like that at all," I answer. "And I think the reason it hasn't come up is because we're still in the very early stages of our relationship. We're still essentially two single guys who are dating—"

"What you're talking about, and where you've gone with Anson, emotionally and sexually, is more than dating," she tells me, in a corrective tone.

Welcoming that, because it validates at long last what I've been thinking about Anson and myself, I say: "We really are, aren't we?"

"Are what?"

"Boyfriends, lovers, that's what Anson and I are."

"And how do you feel about that?" she asks.

That damned feeling question. Therapists ought to just make a cassette recording and punch the play button. "The thing I most feel is appreciative. Grateful and excited and afraid that this is going to change my whole life around."

"We'll see," she says, rather cryptically.

This seems to signal the end of that topic. She shifts in her chair, smoothes the lap of her skirt. I stare at the Persian rug and study the patterns, squares and circles and long flowing curves like delicate arabesques.

"You know," I say, "I wasn't surprised when Scotty told me he'd tested positive. I hadn't expected it — because he's gone so many years without getting infected, and he's very sexually active. But when he told me, the only thing I could think of was that this would be the end of his relationship with Kent—"

"And Kent tested negative again?" she asks.

"Yes, and this whole thing's been a real blow to Kent, to say the least. He came to me, asking what to do. I didn't know what to tell him. 'Do what your heart tells you' is what I said. Pretty lame, I know. Then I got more specific. I told him that if he didn't think he could handle everything that comes with a positive test, then he should think about leaving. He asked me, over and over, 'But should I leave? Get it over with now? I'm not happy about the monogamy thing.'

"That's what he kept asking me, and I kept telling him that he had to make that decision on his own. What else could I say? If I'd urged him to stay, and then he started flipping out and being mean and god-knows-what, then I'd have done Scotty — and Kent — a disservice. If I counseled Kent to go, depriving me of my housemate and friend and depriving Scotty of the love and intimacy and support that he gets from Kent, then I'd feel guilty.

"What it boils down to, I told Kent, is that there are no truly good options available to him. Whichever way he decides to go, there'll be obstacles and difficulties. There could also be great rewards, too.

"I don't think he liked this conclusion, because I don't think he likes accepting that there are no good options available to him. At least from his point of view. We're not talking about deciding between swordfish or chicken for dinner. I think that Kent is a little bit spoiled, and that he's used to always getting his way."

I stop, coming up for air. A cool gentle breeze has come up, now trembling on the edges of the drapes.

"And you say you felt nothing at all about Scotty's testing positive?" she asks, rather rhetorically it seems.

"No, nothing at all," I say. "I'm sure it will catch up with me eventually—"

"That's what I was just going to tell you," she says.

"It seems that all things, all this, the epidemic, the dying, the renewal, the hope — they are all experienced in some mode of delayed response. They do catch up, but sometimes it takes weeks, or months, or years."

She nods solemnly, as though this is great wisdom. She rests her hands, palms up, in her lap. It is a strange, vulnerable gesture.

"What else?" she asks.

"One other thing I wanted to get to is — still — my frustration with therapy. You know, Charlton suggested to me to try spirituality to help change my life. We talked about that last time. What I don't see, is just what I want to change my life to be. But then, we talked about that last time, too."

"Yes, we did," she says. Then suggests, "Why not sit down and make a list of the changes you would like to see in your life — less illness, less grief, a greater sense of purpose, a lifting of depression, wanting a raise at work. Or whatever. That sort of thing."

"Well, I suppose it would be a start. You know, a long time ago, when I was first getting involved with Scotty, it was a real eye-opener for me to discover that he was deeply spiritual in a way I'd never known before, in anyone. Not religion, mind you, but a sense of the one-ness of everything . . . god, do I sound goofy or what? but you know what I mean.

"And he would practice magic, perform certain rituals to attain his goals. I tried these things for a while, and I believe I got some benefit from them. Maybe I should pursue that?"

She nods. "Whatever seems right for you. Remember your time in AA and NA? When you were first getting sober?"

"Of course," I answer.

"Well," she pursues, "you said you followed the twelve steps?"

"Of course I did," I answer, almost defensively (though I'm not sure why).

"Well, the twelve steps are really just a magic system. You perform certain tasks, take certain steps, connect with someone, some strength outside yourself, and things change, like getting cleaned up, getting sober."

"Oh," I say, having never thought of the program in quite this way. "Oh," I say again.

For a few minutes we talk in an idle, unexcited way about Mama Jones and my feelings of dismay at her sudden, serious illness. Dr. Kiljoy tells me, "But there has always been sickness and death." And then I remember her family background, the relatives lost in the gas chambers and ovens of the Third Reich. I do not pursue this line of thought, nor do I continue with any discussion of the seeming unfairness of my life, of life.

Walking home, I run into an old friend, from my early days in the gym, way back at the start of the plague. He is heavily muscled, glowing, and handsome. "Glad to see you're still alive!" he declares. He is so strikingly healthy that I think he must have HIV or even AIDS. The new treatments seem to restore people to better health than they ever had before it all began. "Strange, isn't it?" I say. "I think they're going to have to drive a stake through my heart to get rid of me!" We part, and I feel as though something of the past has survived, has been salvaged, perhaps, by the new hope.

14

On a clear crisp cold day, the sky a blend of bright blue and golden light, Scotty comes home from General Hospital, from his doctor's appointment, with a bagful of medicine bottles. When I enter his room, he has scattered the bottles across the bed and is sitting still and staring, in a haunted way, at the mass of medications. For a long moment I stand in the door, silently, knowing that my presence is as yet undetected. And I examine him, this beautiful boy whom I have loved for so many, many years.

His back is turned to me, displaying the architecture of his torso — his muscular shoulders, the edge of his tattoo showing like a tattered hem at the sleeve of his T-shirt. His thick, athletic neck rises to a perfectly round head, the ears small, the hair a brown so dark it is nearly black. In that moment, in a wistful way, I think, again, I love this boy, and then he turns, sees me standing in the doorway, and simply looks at me. There are tears in his eyes, as yet unshed.

Not knowing what words to choose for this mutual silent heartfelt interaction — our eyes lock, his brimming with tears — I say simply, "That's a lot of pills."

He nods his head. And then wipes the corner of his eye with his hand, and looks down at the pile. "They believe in bombarding the virus with as much as the body can stand, as early as possible. But looking at all this, I don't know . . ."

His voice breaks, and I, suddenly frozen in the doorway, command myself to walk into the room, sit on the edge of the bed, and cradle him in my arms. He cries, in a gentle, uncertain way, and then straightens himself, wipes his cheeks with his fingers. "Look at me, I'm a mess."

"You are not a mess," I tell him. "You're perfectly normal. Do you think anyone gets this sort of news and doesn't cry? What would that be like?"

"But it's not the virus that bothers me, it's all these pills, what they mean, how they'll make me feel, how long it will go on."

"Welcome to the club," I say, trying to sound ironic, or at least sarcastic. But what comes out is a dreadful misery, and then I begin to shed tears. "Now it's my turn to be a mess," I choke out.

And then we both begin to laugh, laughter that grows beyond all proportion. We clutch at our aching stomachs as we howl and roll on the bed. "And to think," Scotty gasps out, trying to stifle the laughter, "Kent's thinking of leaving me and missing out on all this fun!"

We both collapse again in hysteria, quite silly. And quite cathartic. Oh, I'll enjoy telling Dr. Kiljoy about this. She'll be happy that at long last I've shown some emotion, inappropriate as it may be.

◆

I have a horrible three days at work, nothing but lunches with authors, staff meetings, and a press deadline looming over a very troublesome book.

For relief, Anson takes me to San Gregorio Beach, just down the coast from the City, in that gentle landscape of soft green rolling hills, hothouses, artichoke fields, and tiny hamlets. We park the car and make our way down the trail to the beach. The fog is out to sea, and we are blessed with dazzling, blinding sunlight, hot and burning. We choose a "fort" of driftwood, spread our towels, and strip.

Lying there on the beach, with the song of the surf the only sound in my ears, I open my eyes, shield them from the sun with my hand to my forehead, and look up at the jagged, crumbling cliffs, the odd clump of wildflowers here and there, a bit of sea grass sprouting in a sliced ravine.

I hear Anson light a cigarette, and I ask him to light one for me, too. We smoke in silence, drenched in sunshine, no cares, no worries, at least for the moment. I look sidelong at Anson as he gazes out across the ocean. My heart is full when I study his profile, his shiny shaved head, his handsome "roman" nose, his full red lips. I lean over and kiss him.

"Hey, babe," he says, warmly.

"You know," I say, "that I'm in love with you."

He smiles and says, "I know. I love you, too."

He reaches for my hand and we sit like that, smoking and holding hands, filled with magic.

◆

When we leave, gathering up our things, stuffing them into our backpacks, we toss the remnants of our lunch — sourdough bread, a bit of sharp Vermont cheddar, nuts and celery — to the gulls.

We hike up the trail to the dusty parking lot, and as we are loading our packs into the trunk, a great red pickup truck (with a King cab) races into the parking lot, spins around, and begins to roar away. As it does, the youths in the cab give us hateful glares and shout "Fags!"

As if we didn't already know?

Later, when we have napped and had dinner, we sit up in bed watching reruns of *The Brady Bunch*.

"Is this pedestrian entertainment?" I ask (snootishly).

"I don't care, it's the best stuff on TV," Anson says.

Following Dr. Kiljoy's suggestion, I make a list of the changes I want to see in my life. At the top of the list, of course, is "Get Out of Depression." I regard this sentence for a moment, realizing that, with the anti-depressant and the therapy, I am already halfway there. I just need a little nudge to get back to a place where I want to be, someplace where I don't feel horrible when I wake up in the morning.

Next on the list is "Be Able to Enjoy Things/Life Again." And here I recall Dr. Kiljoy's explanation about the difficulty of feeling pleasure that's one of the symptoms of depression. Again, I'm halfway there.

"Diminish/Remove the Grief." Yes, it would be wonderful to somehow wash away all the grief, that pulling from the past, from the dead lovers and friends.

I go on in this vein till I have filled a page with desires, including wanting a raise at work and wanting to buy a new car. When I reach the bottom of the page, I can think of nothing else, so I lay down my pen and light a cigarette, regarding the list in a satisfied, absentminded way.

Will it be possible to change?

When the call comes from Michael, I am stunned by the staggering news.

"It's about Mama," he says, after greeting me in a strained voice.

Suspecting something terrible, I prompt, "What is it? How is she?"

"It's cancer," he answers. "Ovarian cancer. I think the official term is ovarian carcinoma. And the worst part is that it already metastasized, spread through her body. The scans show the cancer has spread to the lungs, too. Her doctor told her that she must have the constitution of an ox to be able to be so sick and yet function."

Thunderstruck, I don't know what to say. "What's next?"

"Total abdominal hysterectomy, the day after tomorrow. And then chemo, immediately, and possibly radiation. But it's not good. The prognosis isn't good. They're going to do what they can, but the disease is already pretty far along."

"Oh, my god," I gasp. "How can this be? I mean, she's been feeling bad, right? And she's been looking sick. But how could it be so bad, so serious, so fast?"

"Well, apparently there were more symptoms than she let on," Michael tells me. "She'd noticed a swelling in her abdomen, but thought it was just water retention. And one of the reasons she's been feeling so fatigued — besides being full of cancer — is because she's severely anemic. The doctor said these are all symptoms they see in ovarian cancer."

"Where is she now? Can I talk to her?"

"She's still in the hospital," Michael answers. "And will be for a while. You could try calling over there, but I wouldn't recommend it. They've got her hooked up to a million tubes and things, and she's being given pain killers—"

"She's in pain?" I cut in.

"Yes, apparently a lot of pain that she wasn't telling us about. Anyway, it's probably better for you to call her after the surgery, give it a couple of days. But they're going to start chemo right away, too, after the surgery."

"Geez," I said, breathless. "This is too much, just too much. I wish there were something I could do."

"There's nothing, at the moment," says Michael. "We just have to wait and see what happens. Thank god she's got a good doctor, and she's getting the best care she can at Presbyterian."

In an uncertain way, I venture: "Michael, how are you taking this? Is there something I can do for you?"

"Well, not really. You know, for the past couple of days, ever since I heard of her diagnosis, I've been feeling much better, stronger and less tired. Maybe it's the Chinese herbs kicking in again. I tell you, I was pretty disappointed to feel so well —

so soon — after starting the Chinese stuff and then go right back downhill. But I seem to be on the mend again."

Relieved, I say, "That's good news, at least—"

"And Thomas is being a saint, taking care of everything. He has some sick leave and vacation time coming — way too much, actually, because you know he's a workaholic and never goes anywhere, never takes a vacation — so he's going to work it out that he can be here half days and at work half days."

"You sure?" I ask. "Won't you need us to help out?"

"I really don't think so," Michael answers in an agitated way. I realize that he must be overwhelmed with solicitations of every kind, to help him, to help Mama, to help Thomas. He's probably sick of it all and wants to be left alone, independent. And especially now, when he's doing better on the Chinese medicines, he must want to exercise a little control over his life, take care of things himself. I don't want to deny him this.

"Well, then," I say, at a loss. "You do know you can call any of us, any time, whatever—"

"Yes, thank you, I know," he says. "And you know I will, if I need it."

"Okay, then . . ."

"Well, I better make some more calls. I'll talk to you later?"

"Okay," I say. "Good-bye."

❖

I hasten to phone Charlton with the news, feeling a little horrified at the excitement I feel. This flip side of crisis — the exhilaration and excitement — is troubling, always. But it is something I have learned to accept, though not without pause.

Charlton, of course, has already spoken with Michael and is as informed as I am. "I'm in shock," he says. I hear the click of his cigarette lighter. "To think that all this time, when Mama's been feeling down, that she's been getting eaten up by cancer . . . cancer of the worst sort, not that there's a good sort of cancer, but you know what I mean, the outlook is pretty bleak . . . it's just plain . . . well . . . shocking."

"It is," I agree. "I think I'm stunned. Of course I want to say I don't believe it, but of course I do. We've lived through too many health emergencies to do the denial thing."

"Yes, yes," he sighs. I hear him exhaling a stream of smoke. "But there's really nothing we can do. I understand Michael's advice that we not visit her, not now. When I was in the hospital, during the worst of my lymphoma, I just wanted to be left alone to rest and cope. I didn't want anyone around, even people I dearly cared about."

"I'm not sure I understand that," I say, "since I've never been sick, really sick—"

"Knock on wood!" Charlton cuts in.

"Yes, knock on wood," I echo.

"And the news couldn't have come at a worse time," he says, adding, in a resigned tone, "but then that's always the way, isn't it?"

"What do you mean?" I ask.

"Well, Derek — what's-his-name to you — has left me—"

"What? Left you?" I say. "That wasn't very long—"

"Oh, thanks," he says. "No it wasn't very long, only a couple of months really. But he left in a really hateful way. I came home from grocery shopping to find his key to my house on the kitchen counter with a terse note saying 'Moving back to Boston. Have a good life.' And that was all. He had taken everything of his out of my place, his clothes, toothbrush, little things mostly. But it really hurt.

"I called him right away, to see if I couldn't figure this out, but his line's been disconnected and there's no forwarding number. Which means he must have been planning to leave for at least a few days, if not longer. It wasn't a snap decision. But he never even hinted that something was wrong, that he was moving back East, or anything. And this morning, I got the call from Michael. This is not a good week."

"What a mess," I say. "But I'm not surprised at the suddenness. Wasn't he just twenty-four or something?"

"Twenty-three."

"Right. And you said he was a party boy, tweaking. That's what those kind of people do, those crystal addicts. Totally unpredictable, in a way. But in another way, sadly, obviously predictable."

"And now you're going to tell me that I'm better off without him," Charlton says, in a bitter way.

"You said it, not me."

"Oh, I guess you're right, I am better without all that energy and drama in my life. What was I thinking, getting involved with a twenty-three-year-old?"

"He was cute," I say simply. "And kind of lovable. And you told me he had a big dick."

"Hmm, yes, he did . . . he does . . . Oh, what the fuck. I'm going to go to my sister's house in Mill Valley and drink myself to sleep. You can call me there if anything changes with Mama or Michael."

"Okay," I agree, hanging up.

When I finally have a few moments alone, I sit on the back deck, look out across the cityscape, and think, trying to take it all in. It's not easy, of course, nothing like Mama's crisis ever is. But we have grown tough skins, we who have endured, survived this plague. What have we learned from it? What can I take from it that could help me understand this horrifying, sudden illness of Mama Jones?

Buddhists say: "Life is suffering." Christians say: "The Lord moves in mysterious ways." I say (simply): I don't understand, not any of it, not life, not illness, not death. Certainly I have become inured to these facts of life — the tough skin again — and certainly I've gone mostly numb. Things don't disturb me as they once did.

But what is the lesson in this? That something happens to everyone? That no one is spared? That we must accept illness and death — no matter how painful or tragic — as perfectly normal? To be expected?

Of course that's one lesson here. There's nothing strange or wrong or unexpected about illness, about death. How many thousands die every day of starvation? Of drought? Civil war? Plagues?

We are given no guarantees.

Still, Mama's cancer seems cruel, tragic. This woman, who has given so much, doesn't deserve this. But then, does anyone ever deserve anything?

Though we may accept sickness and mortality as givens, we're not required to like them. We are not called upon to look with equanimity upon the face of darkness. We may, if we so feel, respond with anger, with dismay, with dread. And we may respond with patience, courage, hope, and belief.

The sun sinks behind Twin Peaks and colors my deck with dusk and shadows. I smoke a cigarette and stare at the City, thinking no more, feeling nothing. It is pure peace.

❖

The next afternoon, Anson comes over. "Mama Jones is in the hospital with ovarian cancer," I tell him. "She had a hysterectomy this morning, and after a bit of recovery, she must undergo chemotherapy and radiation. It's real bad. The cancer has spread to other parts of her body."

"Good god," Anson says. "I don't know her very well, but she always seems so . . . so . . . vivacious! Hysterectomy? Chemo? Radiation? God, what a mess."

I nod my head. "A mess. That's a good way to describe it."

"But how's Michael?" Anson asks.

"Surprisingly good," I say. "It sometimes takes a crisis to bring out the best in people. Michael is one of those kinds of people to rise to the occasion of an emergency. He phoned to tell me that she came through the surgery okay, and he seemed genuinely all right with it."

"Amazing," he says. "He must be doing better on the new stuff?"

"I guess so," I say, in a lost way. "The problem with Michael is that every day — geez, every hour — is different. The disease has done so much damage for so long that I'm not really sure he'll ever get any better. One day up, the next day down. But I keep hoping that the herbs and acupuncture will really work for him."

"Let's hope," Anson says. And then he puts his arms around me and nuzzles his face against my neck. "Let's go for a drive," he suggests, "to the top of Twin Peaks."

"Yes, let's," I agree. "I haven't been up there in a long time."

We grab our jackets and bundle ourselves into Anson's Miata. We park in the lot and stroll downhill just a bit. The air is cold. By the light on the hills, by the crispness of the wind, we know it is autumn on this island of fog. This October chills us as we stand on the side of the green-brown hill below the Sutro Tower, regarding the mirage of the City shrouded in mist.

Anson puts his arm around my waist and pulls me close for warmth. A rough wind carries a damp chill. Gazing out at the hazy cityscape, he whispers "It's beautiful, isn't it?" I nod my head in silent agreement.

He presses his body against my back, and kisses the nape of my neck. "I love you," he tells me. And I echo the same words back to him.

15

Dr. Kiljoy stands at the door to her office and gestures for me to come in. I put down the magazine I'm leafing through and take my seat. She smiles and asks how I'm doing.

"I can never believe how much life happens between these weekly sessions!" I begin.

"A lot going on?" she asks.

"More than a lot. It's unbelievable. I never thought I'd have to deal with something like this now. I always figured it would be Michael who'd go next. Not Cherise."

"Cherise?"

"Mama Jones," I explain. "Her real name is Cherise, and for some reason, I've been thinking about her as Cherise, not as Mama Jones. The very word Mama seems to connote something . . . oh, I don't know . . ."

"You need to bring me up to date. Last week, Mama . . . Cherise . . . was in the hospital for tests. Has there been a diagnosis?"

"Yes," I say, a bit harshly. "It's ovarian cancer. She's already had a complete hysterectomy and will start on chemo and radiation as soon as she's strong enough. But Michael tells me that she isn't recovering from surgery very well. There've been complications, something about her kidneys. The cancer has spread throughout her body, by the way. It doesn't look good. As a matter of fact, Michael tells me that she's in critical condition."

"I see," she says, in a soft tone, a near whisper. "What are you feeling about this?"

Christ!

"Well, overwhelmed, of course, and shocked, and just plain terribly annoyed that something is always going wrong with someone."

Not knowing what to say next, I'm silent. Dr. Kiljoy shifts in her seat and smoothes her skirt. "And how are things going with Scotty?" she asks.

"Oh, about the same, I guess. He started the meds, taking something like sixteen pills a day. Which isn't so bad, really, considering what other guys I know have to take. But to go from zero to sixty, as they say, in a few short days, is pretty hard. He was very upset about it the other day, but something in him changed, just as he started to take the meds. I think he became full of hope that he'll be able to do pulse therapy if he does well on these meds, so he won't have to take pills all the time, every day, forever, so this will be a detour, not the expressway.

"It's really different now, actually. When I found out I was positive, there still wasn't anything to do. It's taken years and years to get to a point where they actually have something to offer, something that works."

"And how does that make you feel?" she asks.

"Hopeful . . . and . . . angry—"

"Why angry?"

"Because it doesn't seem fair that we should have the opportunity to treat the infection when so many of my friends and lovers didn't. There was no hope. I know I should be happy, ebullient even. And I am, in a way. But somehow, when I think about it in a selfish way, you know, thinking only of myself — which I'm very good at doing — it seems grossly unfair."

"But there we are again, life isn't fair," she says. "Life is filled with difficulty, illness, and death. It's the way."

Something in her final sentence sets me on edge. Maybe it's the declarative nature of saying "It's the way," as though she were some sort of guru pronouncing on the nature of life.

But then again, that's exactly what she is. That's the role I've let her play.

By way of finishing about Scotty I say, "He's scheduled for a viral load test in just another two weeks, after he's been on the drugs for three weeks. I expect it to be zero."

"And why is that?" she asks.

"Because everyone I know who's on those drugs . . . everyone except Michael . . . has done, is doing very well on them, getting zero viral loads almost immediately. It's a miracle, isn't it?"

She nods. "Yes, it is." And taking up her notepad, she jots something down, and then says: "By the way, before I forget, I need to let you know that we won't be meeting next time. I'll be having a vacation all next week, so we'll meet again in two weeks. If there's any sort of problem, you can call my number and Dr. Dorfmann will be on call. But I don't suppose you'll need to do that."

"You never know," I say, thinking how odd I suddenly feel knowing that she will be away. It's as if a certain touchstone were being removed from my life just as I'm most in need. But I say nothing about this. What I say is, "Of course that'll be fine. I'll get along okay."

She smiles and nods in a formal way, and I am reminded, once again, of her Old World connections. She can be so damned Viennese! If she were very old (very, very) I'd expect her to have met Freud himself.

"You know," I say, changing the subject, "I made that list you suggested, of the changes I'd like to see in my life and the things I'd like to have. I'm afraid it's not a very long list, just one page, but it seems pretty comprehensive to me. Do you want to read it?"

"No, I don't think that's necessary," she answers. "But what do you plan to do with it?"

"I thought I'd ask you," I say. "What should I do with it?"

"What do you want to do with it?" she asks, circularly. "Perhaps some sort of prayer list or ritual? I don't really know, it's up to you."

"Oh," I say. I'd expected more from her on this. "Well, now . . . let me see . . . Well, Scotty usually lights a candle or two, burns some incense, and makes these requests to the gods or higher powers, or whatever. I suppose I could do something like that."

She nods but says nothing.

"But what do you think?" I ask her, trying, once more, to prompt her into making some suggestions.

"Oh, I wouldn't know," she says. "The important part, really, is what you've already done. Put things clearly on paper. The last part, the last half of it, doesn't much matter. You could simply meditate on these ambitions. Or you could ritualize it all. Or you could examine each item here in therapy, let us focus on how to approach these changes. What is essential, though, is that you gain a sense that there is something beyond psychotherapy, that there's something more than talking that can be effective."

"Really?" I say, in an incredulous tone. "I wouldn't have thought you'd say that. I'd think you'd pooh-pooh the whole idea."

"But not at all," she says. "Not at all."

"Well, if truth be told," I say, in a confessional way, "I've already started to sit quietly and read the list, one item at a time, meditating on each thing. It's strange how spirituality is being reintroduced into my life. But with Scotty's seroconversion, and Mama Jones's illness, it's seemed important, imperative really, that I activate some sense of the spiritual. Where else am I going to get strength?"

"From the love and support of your friends," she says, plainly.

"But isn't that — love — a spiritual thing?"

"Very much so," she answers. "I'm glad to hear you say that."

Is she patronizing me? I wonder.

At a loss, I say, "It's just so strange, I wouldn't have thought it would be Charlton who would get me interested in spiritual things again. I mean, he seems so . . . so . . . profane somehow. As though there's not a sacred bone in his body. And yet he's been to the brink and back more than once. And he's survived lymphoma more than once. I wonder if that means Mama Jones can survive this cancer?"

Saying this as a question, I look, searchingly, at Dr. Kiljoy. Who sits very still and says only, "Perhaps."

"There's always hope, isn't there?" I say. "One thing I've learned from the epidemic is that there's always hope. Not hope in the sense that things can always turn out right, or the way we'd like them to, but the fact that even in the face of staggeringly bad odds, we can still cling to hope. It's an amazing emotion, really."

She nods again, and smiles, then shifts in her chair and smoothes her skirt.

"I guess I'm really rambling today, aren't I? Going from thought to thought. That must mean I'm more upset than I actually know?"

"Not especially, no," she says. "But you're clearly preoccupied, distracted. That's to be expected."

Just then, there is a knock at her door. She sits up for a moment, stiffens, and a frown creases her brow. The knock comes again, and, under her breath, I am sure I hear a faintly whispered "Shit!"

She goes to the door, opens it. There is a young woman with long dark hair, dressed rather well for an afternoon. She mumbles something to Dr. Kiljoy, who says, "I have a client right now. This is not convenient. I'll give you a call later on. Will you be at home?" I hear the girl mutter yes, yes, and then Dr. Kiljoy closes the door, crosses to her chair, and sits down again.

"I'm terribly sorry about the interruption," she says, clearly flustered.

"Oh, it doesn't matter," I say (because it doesn't).

"Where were we?"

"Nowhere, really," I say. "I was just going on about spirituality and stuff like that. I really don't have much to say. Mama's in the hospital, and I think she's dying, and Michael's doing better, for the moment, and Scotty's taking his drugs, and Charlton's boyfriend has dumped him, and I'm in love with Anson, and we're having a great time together. That's about all there is to say.

"I suppose we could pick up the thread about the masculinity stuff, but somehow none of that seems very important right now. I've been thinking about it, though, because I'm starting to notice the masculine traits in the people around me, like Michael's lover Thomas, who is a tower of strength. And Michael's courage, as well as Scotty's, to deal with truly devastating circumstances without flinching, but merely putting the work in that's needed."

"You see 'not flinching' as a masculine characteristic?" she asks.

"No, not really . . . that's funny, as soon as I said it, I thought, well, perhaps flinching, when appropriate, would be a very masculine quality. Not flinching — I mean not having your emotions, or suppressing them, or not expressing them — or not having the courage to express them — would be a childish thing to do, or not do, as the case may be, not manly . . ."

My voice trails off. "I'm talking myself into a corner where I don't remember what I'm saying." I laugh at myself.

She smiles, and almost chuckles. "That's fine," she says, quite reassuringly. "You have important matters on your mind. We'll pick up the thread in a future session."

"Ah, that reminds me," I say in a tentative, unsure way. "I've been thinking that it might be the right thing for me to do to wind down therapy, finish with it for the time being."

She raises her eyebrows. "Oh?"

"It's just that . . . oh . . . it has never felt right somehow. I don't think I've kept it secret that I've had doubts about therapy all along—"

"That's right," she says quickly.

"And I think that having stumbled over this spirituality thing has been the most valuable bit that I'll take from the work we've done. I'd like to focus my attention on that, rather than keep coming back to talk about my troubles, or abstractions like masculinity and such. Would you mind terribly if we stopped altogether?"

"No, I wouldn't mind," she answers. "I just want to be sure you're ready to stop."

"You know, you've been wonderful, and getting on the anti-depressant has been a tremendous help. But, to be blunt about it, I just don't want to keep doing this."

She takes a long, slow breath, lets it out. She cocks her head, as she did during our first visit. She says, "I certainly agree that you've made significant progress. And if you'd like to end therapy, that's fine."

Oh, I think, it's that easy? "Of course, I'd like to be able to come back for a tune-up once in a while, if that's okay?"

"Of course it is," she says. "Anytime."

"Well, I guess that's that," I say, a bit too dismissively. But once I've broached this subject, and found that she has no objections, I'm eager to be on my way, to put this work behind me.

She stands and smiles at me. She extends her hand and says, "It's been my pleasure to work with you. I'm glad that Charlton recommended me. And I wish you very well."

I shake her hand (and are those tears I feel on my eyelids?). "Thank you, too. Good-bye."

When I emerge from her office, I feel light, free. It's a great relief.

16

Kent comes to my room to "talk things over." I'm sprawled across the floor, listening to Marc Almond on the CD. In a lazy, half-interested way, I urge him to tell me what's on his mind.

"Of course, it's the positive test," he says. "I've just had a terrible time trying to reconcile myself to it. And I'll be honest, I really thought that I just couldn't face it, couldn't stand the idea that Scotty's going to get sick and—"

"Scotty's not going to get sick," I interrupt him. "It's no longer a given that someone with HIV is going to get sick. In fact, it never was. There's lots of people around who've been infected now for more than two decades. And with the new drugs..." I stop, then quietly ask, "What are you going to do? Are you going to leave him, leave us?"

"No," he says emphatically, decisively. "I am not going to leave. It's not going to be easy for me, I realize that, but I can't abandon Scotty just because he made a mistake and got infected. What would that say about my values? About my love for him? My commitment to him?"

I nod my head, inwardly smiling. I recognize that this is a turning point for Kent, and I'm proud of him for making what seems to me to be the right decision. "I agree," I say. "I'd think that your love for him would outweigh your fears and anger and uncertainty."

"I hope so," he says. "But it's not going to be easy."

"Oh, please, Kent, it's not all that big a deal. Not anymore. Sure it's serious, but there's a whole shitload of treatments now, and many more on the way. I really believe, now, that they're going to whip this thing, end it soon. There's no reason to get all worked up about it. There's no reason for your life to change, or for your relationship to change, or anything for that matter."

He nods his head, looking pensively out the window. The Marc Almond CD finishes, and I put on the Butthole Surfers, a real change of pace.

Kent is quiet for a few moments. Then he shrugs his shoulders and says, "That's all I wanted to say. I'm going to talk to Scotty when he gets home from work, let him know that I'm behind him a hundred percent."

"I'm proud of you," I say, hoping that I sound supportive, not patronizing. He goes to his room and I turn off the CD and lie down for a nap.

But I can't sleep. For some reason, Kent's decision has resurrected my ghosts — friends and lovers of the past, all who've gone on into the afterworld. It's a matter of perspective. For while it seems that Kent's decision has great impact — on Scotty, on me — in the long run it amounts to very little.

But then again, that's true of just about everything. Yet I lie there, hearing a dog bark next door, hearing the rush of wind through the sycamores outside the bedroom window, and I see faces, phantoms from the past, all laughing and partying and dancing and fucking.

Eventually, drifting into sleep, I dream, half awake, of these men and their short, shortened lives, and they come to me, these spirits, and dance for me in my waking dream. I miss them all, terribly. I'm glad that Kent is going to rally for Scotty, and I miss these lost lives.

◆

Michael phones. I am relaxing, catching a few moments of absolutely nothing, listening to Enya.

"I'm afraid it's not good news," Michael tells me. "Mama is not recovering from her surgery very well. She's in critical condition, in the intensive care unit. As a matter of fact, she's doing worse than that. The problem with her kidneys is serious, very serious, and she's just not recuperating at all. There's no way they can start chemo while she's so sick. They don't know what's going to happen."

"Jesus Christ," I say, futilely. "I better go see her."

"They won't let you in," he says. "She's in intensive care, and there are no visitors allowed. At least not right now."

"Well, then, I'll call her," I say.

"She can't answer the phone either," he tells me, going on: "They've got her on two separate IVs, she's intubated to help her breathe. As a matter of fact, she's on life support." And then, as his voice breaks, Michael says, "I don't think she's going to make it."

"Good Lord," I say.

"Stop saying that," Michael pleads. "I don't think Jesus Christ or the Good Lord can help her now." He chokes these words out, and I realize that he's weeping.

"Oh, Michael, I'm sorry," I say. "Is Thomas home?"

"No, this is his afternoon at the office," Michael answers, a bit more coherently.

"Then I'm coming over right now," I say, "because you shouldn't be alone."

"None of us should be alone," he says. "But I'd be glad if you came over, just to hold my hand and keep me company."

◆

As I'm putting on my jacket to go, Scotty arrives in an ebullient mood. "My viral load is zero," he announces, in an excited, triumphant way.

◆

When I get to Michael's flat, he buzzes me in, and as I climb the stairs, I'm shocked by his appearance. Another severe downturn, I see. Shit. Not now. Not with all this other stuff going on.

"Hello, Tiger," I say, in a tone that attempts to be chipper, but is, in fact, strained.

"Tiger? What is this, a football game?"

"Sorry," I apologize. "I was trying to be cheerful."

"Why on earth would you try to be cheerful now?" Michael asks, his tone incredulous, angry even.

"Well, I don't know . . ." I say, lamely. "How should I be? Weeping and tearing at my clothes?"

"No sarcasm, please," he says, "I can't take it right now."

I decide, judiciously, to change my tone. Apparently Michael is in need of sober, somber company, so I offer to make him a drink.

"I couldn't possibly drink anything," he says, "I think I'd throw up. But you go ahead and have something."

"Oh, no, I'm trying to be sober again," I say.

"Well, a little nip wouldn't matter," he says.

"That's okay," I say, "I'll just have a Coke. You want one?"

"Yes, that sounds good," he says, sitting himself back down in the overstuffed corduroy chair — his throne it has become, where, with legs propped up on the ottoman, remote control in hand, he rules his world.

"Is there something I can do?" I ask, handing him his Coke.

"No, nothing," he answers. And then, in a thoughtful, distracted way, he says, "How many times have we been here before?"

"Where?" I ask. "In what way?"

"With a good friend in the hospital, me sick again. Think we've done it ten times, twenty?"

"Well, there was David, first, and then Andrew and Colin and Elliott — the year of the preppies, we called it, remember? And then Powell, Stack, Matt, Kevin, Danny, Denny, Catherine . . . God that was just in the nineties, after we'd become friends . . . It must be about fifteen times already."

"Oh, hell, who cares?" he says, shrugging and flicking the remote, bringing up VH1, which, at that moment, is playing some Mariah Carey video.

"Ugh, mute! Mute it!" I command. "God she makes me sick."

"Me too," Michael says, changing the channel completely, going to A&E, where an Agatha Christie mystery is just beginning. Hercule Poirot is peering into a mirror, adjusting the tips of his moustache. "I love these shows," Michael says.

So we sit and watch the program, drinking our Cokes. All seems well, but Michael is visibly ill — shiny forehead, coughing, too many deep breaths (or are they sighs?). I've seen him like this before, but there's something different, something more, something darker than I've ever seen before. There is an ashen look to his skin — a pallor, really — and a certain dimness in his eyes.

But I don't dwell on these observations. I focus on the mystery at hand, as Hercule Poirot lectures Captain Hastings on some fine point of etiquette. There's nothing I can do for Michael, nothing more than has already been done. It's a matter of time, really. But then, everything is a matter of time these days.

◆

Two days pass, and then, after work, I hear a message, from Michael, on my answering machine: "They've just moved Mama to a hospice, and her medications are being withdrawn. There's no more hope. We can visit her there if we want to, but, apparently, she isn't recognizing anyone, nothing, not even her doctor or her surroundings. I can't talk more. That's it."

As October wears down, with its alternating crystal days and dirty haze, my pace drops to what is, thankfully, something slower, more gentle. Darkness comes early, darkness with its ability to melodramatize even the simplest things. Walking home after work, I see the glowing streetlamps in relief against the gathering darkness, the shine of storefront windows displaying the coming winter's fashions. I stroll along, savoring this slackened mood. These early evening hours are some of the few that I have to myself.

One crisp, smoky evening, Thomas calls to tell me that Michael is still doing poorly. As if in response to Mama's impending death, Michael's decline is extraordinary, and according to Thomas, "Michael's saying things like 'All in all, I've had a pretty good life,' or 'It seems the end may be in sight,' or, more often, 'I guess the party's over.'"

We don't know what to make of this — except, of course, the obvious. But we have seen Michael in this state of mind — and state of health — so many times over the years that we've lost count. "He's not going to make it this time" has been uttered so often it has become something of a dark joke among our group.

Still, according to Thomas, there is a new attitude of acceptance on Michael's part, as he is talking about his "losing, lost battle" with AIDS. Michael says, often, "Let's face it, we're on the wrong end of the food chain now."

But yes, it's true, the days that Michael is sick are far outnumbering the days when he feels marginal. Gone are the days when he actually feels okay.

"Oh, Thomas," I say, "I know we've been at this juncture before, and Michael always pulls through. Don't you think it's just another one of those, another false alarm?" I try to infuse this question with a sense of hope (though dim). But what comes through, in my tone, is an emotion of doom, of calamity just up ahead.

"No, it's not a false alarm," Thomas says, "not this time. Mama's illness, and her move to the hospice, has completely undone him. I really think it's over."

"As many times as we've been through this, with as many friends and acquaintances as we've had," I say, "there's still no good words to offer."

"I know, I know," Thomas wearily says. "I just thought you should know.

"Thank you," I say, hanging up.

◆

The phone rings. It's Charlton. "Hello dolly!" he sings out. "I've got the most terrific news!"

"Oh, good!," I say, honestly relieved that it is not one of the dreaded calls I'm coming to expect (again) these days. "I could use some good news."

"Well, you knew I was going to go to Milan for a press check next month, right?"

"I remember you saying something about—"

"Well, I just talked to Duncan, in New York, and he's agreed to meet me in Milan for a week. Said he'd be interested in talking things over, seeing if we can get back together maybe. Isn't that the best news?"

"Yes, it is," I say, picturing Duncan in his bikini swimsuit from the winter we all went to Key West together. He was — is — a beautiful, beautiful man, blond of course, the way Charlton likes them. That he and Charlton had separated after twelve years together had always been an odd mistake, I thought.

"Do you think you really could?" I ask.

"Could what?" he asks.

"Get back together with him?" I say.

"Oh, of course. Of course. I've never stopped loving him. It was him who had the hangups about a long-distance relationship and all that nonsense. I think he's just coming round to his senses, that's all."

"Well, then, I'm all for it," I say, already envisioning Duncan and Charlton racing in a rented Alfa Romeo along some lofty Italian road. "Send me a postcard."

Overcast skies, cold wind, rain, restless nights. If ever I needed spiritual strength, it is now. I sit at the window, as I do when I'm distraught, and study the brooding sky.

I'd thought, once the new treatments were upon us — and working so well for so many — and after I'd lost the third or fourth generation of friends, that, somehow, the epidemic would slacken, lighten up. To find things otherwise, to wake trembling in the night, to lie in the darkness and hear the baneful wail of the foghorns on the bay, to force myself out of bed, dreading the day — this is not what I envisioned life would be.

Anson sends me a wonderful, warm e-mail:

Life is full of magic, especially when you're in love. As I am with you. What do you think of that? I'm sending this by e-mail, because I want you to have time to think about it before saying either yes or no. Or maybe, not now but later. I think it's time we started thinking about moving in together, either me into your place, or you into mine. Both of us have plenty of room, so it wouldn't be hard to do. And then we'd be together and not have to run all over the place to see each other. And, of course, this isn't just a housing proposition. This is the real thing. You could call it an offer of marriage, but then, you can't make a marriage offer through e-mail, can you? Well, why not? Anyway, I love you that much, and I know (hope?) that you love me, too, enough to want to live together. It would improve my life immeasurably, as being with you in general has already done. I love you. XOXOXO.

It is Halloween. On this night, every year, the Castro fills with men, women, and children in costumes — outrageous drag queens to tiny vampires — all cavorting and howling and having a wild, wild time. For years I have avoided this mess, because the neighborhood becomes so congested that it's nearly impossible to move.

So I've settled myself into the couch, with a good book — Brodkey — and a bowl of popcorn. Scotty and Kent are out somewhere, probably a costume party, so I have the flat to myself.

Just as I throw a blanket over my feet, Anson phones, invites me to spend the night at his place. "But the crowds!" I protest, but the mischievous tone in his voice stirs me, makes me swell with desire.

I accept, eagerly. I grab my overnight bag. I put on my shoes. I open the door and go out.

About The Author

PAUL REED is the author of more than a dozen books, including the novels *Facing It* and *Longing*. His nonfiction work ranges from memoirs and humor to essays on AIDS and health. His short stories, reviews, and essays have appeared in numerous journals and anthologies, including *Black Sheets, The Advocate, The San Francisco Chronicle, The Bay Area Reporter, University Journal,* and the collections *Stolen Kisses* and *Pulp Friction*. Writing under the penname of Max Exander, he has authored five volumes of erotica. Mr. Reed holds a Master of Arts degree in social anthropology from the University of California at Davis. For a decade, he worked as a book editor at the Berkeley publishing firm Ten Speed Press. Since 1991, he has been disabled with AIDS. A native Californian, he divides his time between San Francisco, Healdsburg, and Miami. He can be reached via the website www.paulreed.com.

About The Series

THE SAN FRANCISCO AUTHORS SERIES, published by Black Books, has been established to promote and give voice to the many fine alternative and literary authors in the San Francisco Bay Area. This novel represents the inaugural volume of the series.